BIFOCAL

by
Deborah Ellis
and
Eric Walters

Fitzhenry & Whiteside

First published in paperback in the United States in 2008

Published in Canada by Fitzhenry & Whiteside, 195 Allstate Parkway, Markham, Ontario L3R 4T8

Published in the United States by Fitzhenry & Whiteside, 311 Washington Street, Brighton, Massachusetts 02135

www.fitzhenry.ca   godwit@fitzhenry.ca

Library and Archives Canada Cataloguing in Publication

Ellis, Deborah, 1960-
    Bifocal / Deborah Ellis and Eric Walters.

ISBN 978-1-55455-036-4 (bound)   ISBN 978-1-55455-062-3 (pbk.)

I. Walters, Eric, 1957– II. Title.

PS8559.L5494B53 2007   jC813'.54   C2007-902285-5

**U.S. Publisher Cataloging-in-Publication Data
(Library of Congress Standards)**

Ellis, Deborah, 1960–
Bifocal / Deborah Ellis and Eric Walters

[72] p. : col. photos. ; cm.
Summary: When a Muslim boy is arrested at a high school on suspicion of terrorist affiliations, growing racial tensions divide the student population.

ISBN 978-1-55455-036-4   ISBN 978-1-55455-062-3 (pbk.)

1. Muslims – Civil rights – Juvenile fiction. 2. Race relations – Fiction – Juvenile literature. I. Walters, Eric, 1957– II. Title.
[Fic] dc22   PZ7.E4457B   2007

 Canada Council   Conseil des Arts   ONTARIO ARTS COUNCIL
for the Arts   du Canada   CONSEIL DES ARTS DE L'ONTARIO

Fitzhenry & Whiteside acknowledges with thanks the Canada Council for the Arts, and the Ontario Arts Council for their support of our publishing program. We acknowledge the financial support of the Government of Canada through the Book Publishing Industry Development Program (BPIDP) for our publishing activities.

Design by Fortunato Design Inc.
Cover image by Wes Lowe

Printed in Canada

10 9 8 7 6 5 4 3 2 1

To those we have been told to fear

CHAPTER ONE
JAY

"SEVEN!" they all yelled as I pushed the barbell up, locking my arms to full extension.

I lowered it down, my arms almost buckling under the weight. Lowering it slowly was just as hard as lifting it. I took a breath and exhaled through my mouth as I thrust my arms upward again. My left arm began to shake, and I could feel it lag slightly behind the right—

"You can do it, Jay! You can do it!" Kevin shouted.

I pushed harder and locked both arms into a full extension.

"Eight!" they all screamed. There were at least fifteen people in the weight room. Every last one of them had stopped lifting and now stood around me, watching, cheering, and predicting whether I would make it.

I held the weight motionless for a second before allowing it to drop to just above my chest once again.

"Two more to go," one of the guys said.

"He's not gonna be able to do it," another one added. "He's a line*backer*, not a line*man*."

1

I tried not to think about what they were saying. I couldn't think about anything except the weight pressing against my chest. I took a deep breath and exhaled violently as I pushed the bar up with all my might.

"Nine!" everybody yelled.

I held it at full extension—all two hundred and twenty-five pounds of it—for a good second. It was easier to hold it up with my arms locked than let it back down. As slowly as possible, I lowered it, making sure I still had enough control to keep it from slamming down on my chest.

"One more to go, Jay," Kevin said. "You're going to do it. That's an order!"

Kevin wasn't joking about it being an order. He was captain of the football team and was used to people doing what he told them to do.

"I know you can do it!" he yelled.

If he could have felt the burning in my muscles and the weakness in my arms, he wouldn't have been so confident.

"He's done!" one of the linemen called out. "He's done like dinner!"

He was hoping. Linebackers weren't supposed to outlift linemen, *especially* not a grade-eleven linebacker outlifting a grade-twelve lineman.

"Do it, Jay!" Kevin screamed. "Do it!"

I held the weight in place, just above my chest, trying to gather enough strength for one more lift.

2

"Jay...Jay...Jay..." Steve, the assistant captain started chanting. The others joined in. "Jay...Jay... Jay!"

I took a deep breath, exhaled, and with all of my remaining strength pushed the weight up, my arms fully extended and locked in place. Some of the players cheered, led by Kevin.

I'd done it! I'd bench-pressed two hundred and twenty-five pounds ten times. All I had to do was lower the bar into the guards and—no. That wasn't the end.

I let the weight come straight down until it just hovered over my chest. Without resting, I thrust it back up into the air, locking it in place for the eleventh lift.

The room exploded. Nobody had expected it, which made it even sweeter. I would have laughed out loud myself if holding the weight weren't taking up every bit of my energy.

"I got it!" Kevin said as he grabbed the bar and helped me ease it into the guards. "No point in busting a gut!"

It felt as if more than just two hundred and twenty-five pounds had been lifted off my chest. It was the weight of the entire team—those who wanted me to make it and those who—

"Cops!" somebody cried as he barged through the door to the weight room. "There are cops in the school!"

3

"Big deal," Kevin said. "There are always cops in the school."

Cop cars were often parked in front of the school. This was a big school, and it seemed like there was always something happening. Back at my old school, the cops only showed up to watch one of the teams play.

"Not just cops. *Lots* of cops—dozens of them. They're everywhere!"

Suddenly my eleven lifts didn't seem that important. For a split second, everybody just stood there, frozen in place.

All at once, the group rushed for the door. I jumped off the bench and followed along with the herd. My arms felt like spaghetti but my legs were fine.

There were lots of people in the hall. It was two-thirds of the way through lunch and kids were at their lockers or milling around—although, really, nobody was standing still. The hall was like a river that flowed toward the front foyer. Whatever there was to see must be happening right there at the front doors. I moved along with the guys from the team, wondering what could bring so many cops to the school. It had to be a fight. Or a huge drug bust.

"Clear the way!" a voice boomed out.

Kids veered away from the center of the hall—like the parting of the Red Sea—as two hulking cops strode side by side, right toward us. They weren't just regular cops. They were wearing thick bullet-proof vests and helmets, and one of them was holding a shotgun!

I stared at them, frozen. Kevin grabbed me and pulled me off to the side a split second before they marched past. Nobody spoke. The only sound was the noise of their heavy boots echoing down the hall.

Their uniforms were all black. Even the insignias on their sleeves were just a different shade of black. Both men had guns on their hips with another gun strapped to the side of their black boots.

As the cops continued down the hall, the center remained slightly open in their wake. The students who had been moving in one direction all started being drawn in the other as they followed the cops. The silence was replaced by dozens and dozens of voices all talking at once.

"You ever seen cops like that before?" I asked.

"Maybe on TV or something," Kevin said. "Like those SWAT guys in the movies."

"But why would they be here?"

"I don't know, but we're going to find out. Come on." He started off in the opposite direction—away from where the police were headed.

"Where are we going?" I asked as both Steve and I followed. Everybody else in our group had been pulled along by the crowd.

"We need to see things from the outside."

Kevin wasn't armed like the cops were, but he was big enough to clear a space as he moved against the flow. Kids got out of his way, and the opening remained clear for Steve and me to follow. The guys on the football team could always move people out of the way. Some of the players really liked doing that. I had to admit that I got a charge out of it myself.

Kevin skidded to a stop and we almost bumped into him. Two more cops—regular looking officers— blocked the doors ahead of us. Nobody could leave the school by that exit until they were checked briefly, and then pushed out the door.

"What now?" Steve asked Kevin.

"We're not going that way. If they kick us out, we'll never find out what's happening. Follow me," he ordered.

Kevin led us up the stairwell, still against the flow of traffic. We were the only ones going up. Kevin carved out a channel along one wall, and the crowd moved aside. Up and around, landing by landing to the second floor...then to the top floor. The hallway was almost deserted.

Kevin jumped up into the air. Before I could even think to question what he was doing, he grabbed a ladder suspended against the ceiling. One side came down on a spring, as the other end remained anchored to the ceiling. I'd been in this corridor a

6

hundred times but had never noticed that ladder.

On the ceiling was a sign that read Authorized Personnel Only.

Kevin ignored the sign and started up the ladder. At the top was a small trapdoor. He shoved it open and a square of light appeared over our heads.

Kevin climbed through the opening and onto the roof. Steve immediately scrambled after him. I was next in line. I didn't know if this was such a bright idea, but I really wanted to see what was going on. I started up the ladder.

"Attention!" the PA barked out. It was our principal, Mr. Atkins. "We are in a lockdown."

Lockdown. We had to get into a classroom, away from the windows and behind a locked door. Lockdowns were for emergencies, like somebody waving a gun. My mind raced to thoughts of Columbine...deranged kids killing other students... didn't they kill guys who were on the football team? A sick feeling erupted in my stomach.

"All staff and students report to the nearest secure room!" Mr. Atkins barked. He was trying to sound calm, but it wasn't working. "This is not a drill! I repeat. This is not a drill! Everyone report to lockdown locations immediately!"

I froze in place on the ladder, one hand on the rung above my head—three rungs from the top and about the same distance from the bottom. I had to get to the nearest class, turn off the lights, close and lock the door, and—

"Hurry up!" Kevin hissed at me, peering down from the opening.

"It's a lockdown!" I yelled, thinking he hadn't heard the announcement.

"I heard. Get up here now so we can close the door! Consider this our lockdown spot."

I scrambled up the remaining steps. As I pulled myself up, I could feel an ache in my arms; they were still stinging from the weights. Kevin offered me a hand and practically pulled me off the ladder and onto the roof. With my weight gone, the spring of the ladder pulled it back to the roof and it hit with a loud metallic thud, causing me to startle.

Kevin laughed. "You gotta cut back on the caffeine." He gave the trapdoor a shove with his foot and it fell back down with a thud, closed.

"Are you sure we should be up here?" I asked.

"I'm up here all the time."

"They let you do that?"

"I've never asked, and nobody has ever caught me. Until I'm told I shouldn't, I do. Besides, what are they going to do, suspend me?"

"They could."

Both he and Steve laughed.

"Not a chance," Kevin said. They won't suspend me unless I kill somebody."

"If you did kill somebody, you'd be suspended for only a couple days," Steve added with a grin. "No way they'd suspend the captain or any assistant captain of the football team—at least, not during football season."

"Besides, we're just doing what we were told. This is a lockdown. What place could be safer than the roof?" Kevin asked.

I guess he had a point. There was no way that anybody could come up and get us—unless they were already up here. I scanned the roof anxiously. Didn't snipers go up onto roofs so they could pick off people below? I felt instant relief when I realized that there was nobody here but the three of us. Just gravel and tar, a few smokestacks, and a big metal box—some kind of cooling or heating unit sitting in the center of the roof. Sometimes there was a thin line between being imaginative and being paranoid.

Steve was off to the side, bent over, hiding behind and peering over the low wall that surrounded the whole roof. He turned around and waved for us to come over.

"You gotta see this!" he hissed at us over his shoulder.

We moved in, one on each side of him. I was glad there was a wall at the edge. I was no fan of heights, not even three stories' worth of height. I poked my head over the top and gasped. At least a dozen police cars were stopped in the parking lot and in front of the school, lights flashing. Some of them had their doors still open, as if the cops had rushed off so quickly they didn't have time to close them. No cops in sight. I could hardly believe my eyes. It was like a scene from a movie.

"There's more over here!" Kevin called out. I'd been so intent on the scene that I hadn't noticed that he'd moved to the corner of the building.

"I'll check over on the far side," Steve offered. He got up and started running across the roof, gravel crunching under his feet.

I went over to Kevin. At least six more cars had pulled up onto the sidewalk and were blocking all three of the side exits.

"Why would they need this many cops for anything? What's going on?" I asked.

Kevin shook his head. "They got enough guys with guns for World War Three. And do you see those vans?"

One van had on its side in big white lettering: Special Weapons and Tactics. How many of them would fit in a vehicle like that, and, more important, what was happening that couldn't be handled by the regular cops? The more we saw, the less sense any of this made.

"Do you see what's written on that van?" Kevin asked.

"Yeah. Special Weapons and—"

"No. The other one. It says, Bomb Disposal!"

The hairs on the back of my neck went up. If there was a bomb disposal truck, that had to mean that there was a bomb...or at least somebody thought there was a bomb.

"Now it's all making sense," Kevin said.

"What do you mean?"

"Somebody probably phoned in a bomb threat because they didn't want to go to class. That happens all the time."

"And do they react this way all the time, sending in the SWAT guys, and a bomb disposal truck, and dozens and dozens of police? And look—an ambulance."

As we watched, an ambulance entered the parking lot and came to a stop beside the vans.

"Somebody must be hurt," Kevin said. "Or maybe they think somebody *could* get hurt. I guess this is more than a phone threat," he admitted.

There was a growing crowd of kids out on the field—at least a hundred or more. Probably people who'd been let out before lockdown, or who had gone out for lunch and now couldn't get back into school. I wished I'd gone out—or gotten out. Three officers were herding the crowd farther away from the school. What was happening that was so dangerous? Whatever it was, we would have been better off out there instead of up here.

11

What if it *was* a bomb? How were we supposed to get away?

"Here comes a TV truck," Kevin said.

I turned around. A big truck with a satellite dish on its roof was racing into the parking lot. It squealed to a stop right in front of the main doors. It had barely stopped when the doors flew open and two men jumped out, one with a camera on his shoulder. They'd traveled no more than a few feet before they were stopped by two policemen. There was no way I could hear what they were saying, but there was a lot of waving of arms. They were probably going to make the TV crew get back in their truck and—

But no. The cameraman and reporter followed the officers toward the school. I leaned over the little wall so I could watch them. The height made my stomach do a little flip. I grabbed onto the wall with both hands, but I kept watching until they disappeared through the front doors.

At the same time, two other men climbed out of the news truck. One went into the back while the other climbed a little ladder leading up to the roof. Within seconds, he started to raise a satellite tower. They were getting ready to broadcast, live, from right here. People thousands of miles away would know more about what was going than we did.

A second news truck came into the parking lot. It

rounded the curve so fast it looked like two of the wheels almost came off the ground. It squealed to a stop right beside the first and another man jumped from the vehicle, hoisting a big camera onto his shoulder.

"Look!" Kevin exclaimed.

A line of the black-suited cops came marching out of the school. They towered over two students, who were crowded in the middle. Each kid was cuffed, his arms held by an officer on each side. A teacher— it looked like Ms. Singh—was walking beside them, yelling. Then one of the students was pulled out of the group, his cuffs removed.

The news guy rushed forward, his camera on his shoulder, aimed at the procession. He had practically moved his way right into the line before one of the officers waved him back and he stopped moving, his camera following their path.

They led the kid who was still cuffed to a police car and he was shoved inside.

"Could you tell who it was?" I asked.

"I thought I recognized one of them. I think he's in my grade. Both of them were brown," Kevin said.

That much I could see, but I didn't recognize them either. But then again, from this distance and angle, I didn't know if I would recognize my own mother.

"Up on the roof!" came out a loud amplified voice. I practically jumped out of my skin. Somebody had seen us! Instinctively, we both slouched down out of sight.

"This is the police. Stand up and identify your-selves!" called out the voice. "Hands above your head!"

For a split second I couldn't understand what the voice was saying, what he meant. And then it came to me. They had to make sure we weren't dangerous, that we didn't have any weapons!

Slowly I raised my hands and struggled to get to my feet. Kevin grabbed my shirt and pulled me back down with a thud, my hands still up and my face hit-ting against the gravel, which bit into my skin.

"What are you doing?" I demanded.

"What are *you* doing?"

"I'm just trying—"

"You were just trying to be stupid! Come on!"

He crawled off on all fours across the gravel. He jumped to his feet as soon as he was away from the edge of the roof and couldn't be seen from below. Steve was coming from the far corner as well, running.

Kevin grabbed the trapdoor and pulled it open. "Come on!" he screamed at me.

I unfroze, and scrambled as fast as I could on all fours, the gravel stinging my knees and hands before I jumped up and started running. Steve was already down the ladder.

"Hurry up!" Kevin exclaimed.

I tripped down the ladder, grabbing the lip of the trapdoor to stop myself from tumbling headfirst the whole way down. I jumped down the last four steps, practically landing on Steve, who was waiting at the bottom. There was a loud slam as Kevin closed the trapdoor. He climbed down one step, jumped, landed, and rolled forward. Above him, the ladder sprang up and smashed against the ceiling.

Kevin bounced to his feet and we ran through the third floor hall. It was completely deserted.

Steve grabbed the handle of the first door. It was locked.

We had to get out of the hall before the police caught us. If they saw us here, they'd know we were the ones on the roof.

"In here!"

Kevin held a door open. Steve and I ran, bumping into each other as we both tried to go through the door at the same time. I tripped and fell into the room. Kevin slammed the door closed, turned the lock, and flicked off the lights.

We were in the dark.

"We're safe," Kevin said. "At least from the cops."

"We shouldn't have done that," I huffed, trying to catch my breath. "We shouldn't have run from the cops."

15

"We had no choice," Kevin said. "Do you know how much trouble we would have been in if we'd been caught up there?"

"Not nearly as much trouble as we'd be in for running from the police."

"You're wrong. You don't get in any trouble for *running* from the police. You get in trouble for being *caught* running from the police."

"Yeah, man. Relax," Steve said. "We *didn't* get caught."

He was right. We hadn't got caught. At least not yet.

I sat there on the floor, slumped over, and tried to catch my breath. I couldn't believe what we'd just done.

Kevin went over to the door. He pressed his face against the little window and peered out into the corridor.

"Can you see anything?" I asked.

"Nothing. Nothing at all." He sounded frustrated.

Maybe not knowing was frustrating to Kevin. For me, sitting here in the dark was just fine. I was grateful that nobody could see my arms and legs shake.

Kevin nudged me. "You gotta admit that was pretty cool. Right?"

I nodded. "Pretty cool."

Chapter Two

HAROON

"ATTENTION! We are in a lockdown. All staff and students report to the nearest secure room!"

The principal's voice booms over the PA and interrupts our *Reach for the Top* coach, Ms. Singh, in the middle of a lightning round.

"This is not a drill! I repeat. This is not a drill! Everyone report to lockdown locations immediately!"

We can hear students scramble to get out of the hallway.

Ms. Singh turns off the classroom lights, locks the door, and directs everyone to the floor without missing a beat.

"Haroon, name three tributaries of the Mississippi."

The principal repeats his order. I pause before giving my answer to give him time to stop talking.

"You just lost that point," Ms. Singh says. "Distractions are no excuse." Then she's on to the next kid, the next question.

Ms. Monalisa Singh spent a year teaching high school in the Gaza Strip. A high school lockdown in the suburbs does not impress her.

There are six of us students in the classroom, four members of the team and two alternates. I am an alternate. This is the first practice since the team was chosen. Ms. Singh insists on us all drilling together. "One of you is sure to break a leg or fall in love or move to Siberia. I need you all fighting ready."

There is no difference between this drill and the last, but I'm on the outside again, and that makes it feel different to me. José is the other alternate. The real team, the one that will be on television in November—barring romance, broken bones, or relocation to far-flung places—is made up of Azeem, Nadia, Marie, and Nygen. We meet twice a week, gobble down our bag lunches while watching videos of old shows, then go right into the drills. Ms. Singh is rigorous. By the time lunch hour is over, my brain is always tired but energized at the same time.

"You hesitate too much over your answers," Ms. Singh had said when she kept me after comparative religions to inform me that I was an alternate. "You know what's right, but you don't trust yourself."

I couldn't argue with her about that. "Often I can see the answer in front of me, but I start to question it. How can I be so sure it's right? Isn't that just arrogance? And what if the answer is wrong?"

"If it's wrong, it's wrong," Ms. Singh had answered. "This is a quiz show, not the United Nations Security Council. A wrong answer will not

18

make the lights go out, the building collapse, or the crops fail. Use some perspective, Haroon."

For practice, we arrange the desks in a row, side by side—the way we will be on the show. Ms. Singh doesn't stand still behind the podium, though. She bounces around, firing her questions.

"I used to be six feet tall," she joked one day in religions. "Ten years of teaching have worn me down to the little stump you see before you."

She's not a stump. She's five feet, four inches. I know that because she is shorter than my twin sister, Zana, who is five feet, six inches. I'm five feet, ten inches. I'm thinking about people's height when I should be paying attention to Ms. Singh's questions.

She's supposed to be whispering, I guess so the gunman, or whatever threat we're supposed to pretend is in the halls, doesn't know anyone is in here. She's not whispering, though. And she's not down on the floor with us. She's continuing her usual high-powered dance through the lightning round—called snappers on the show—throwing out questions on math and science, geography, history, astronomy, and popular culture, without looking at notes. She teaches sociology, but her brain is a trap for all sorts of information.

With Ms. Singh taking the whole thing so lightly, it's hard for me to take the lockdown seriously. We've had a practice run, and the principal did say this was for real, but probably that just means he wants us out of the way so the drug squad can check some guy's locker for marijuana without giving warning to other drug users to hide their stuff. It could also mean that he's trying to impress a visiting school board official. It could also mean he just wanted a few minutes of quiet in the halls. Lunch hour can get pretty noisy in a school with nearly two thousand students.

We keep drilling. I get my focus back and we zoom from one question to another, one kid to another. No worries about drug raids in this group. Our brains matter too much to us.

She draws an equation on the board, and that's when we hear it. Faint at first, but growing quickly stronger. The rhythm of boots on cement, pounding the floor—tough and powerful.

"Sounds like the football team has escaped again," Ms. Singh laughs. She doesn't have much use for violent sports. There's enough violence in real life, she often tells us. Can't we have grace in our recreation?

We turn our attention back to the board. The boots keep coming.

Then there is a loud banging on the door.

"Perhaps they're looking for recruits," Ms. Singh jokes. It really is a joke because we're quite a geeky-looking lot. I'm the most athletic in the room, but only because my sister keeps dragging me out on the basketball court so she can prove how much better she is at it than I am.

"Police! Open up!"

"We're all safe in here!" Ms. Singh calls out, making no move toward the door.

"Ms. Singh, this is Principal Atkins. Unlock the door."

"But that's against lockdown procedure," she calls back.

There's a lot of huffing and puffing outside the door. We hear a key in the lock. Of course the principal has a master key.

And then the room is full of police. Not the regular blue police. These officers are all dressed in black, with rifles and helmets and visors pulled down over their faces so that we can't see their features.

They go straight for Azeem and for me. We are lifted up and pushed down again, flat on the floor, face down. My nose lands on Nadia's foot. She gently lifts my head and puts it back on the floor.

All of this takes maybe two seconds. I don't have time to yell or protest.

Ms. Singh is going crazy. "Get your hands off my students! Where is your warrant? How can you let this happen?"

I guess that this last question is aimed at the principal, but she doesn't give him any time to answer.

21

"We are training for *Reach for the Top*. Is that illegal now? If so, you'd better take me, too."

On and on she goes, getting in everybody's way. The police try to lift me up, but she puts her foot right down on my back.

"You are not taking these boys away. They are good students and have done nothing wrong."

After a year in Gaza, Ms. Singh is not easily intimidated. Or maybe she was that way before she went to Gaza. Maybe that's *why* she went.

She's pushed off of me and held back. I am lifted up by my arms, which hurt because they are not in a natural position. Someone snaps handcuffs on me. Azeem is fighting, kicking out at the officers, squirming hard to get away. But he's not any taller than Ms. Singh is, and the black-suited men hold him easily.

I look at where the faces should be on my captors, but the visors are so shiny that I just see my own face reflected back. I'm distraught to find that I am crying.

They half drag, half carry us out of the classroom. Ms. Singh ignores both the principal's and officers' orders and comes with us, arguing with each step. I can see faces staring at us through the classroom windows. I feel a terrible weight of shame, even though I haven't done anything wrong.

Down the stairs we are dragged, Ms. Singh nipping at the heels of the police officers.

In the front hall, there are many more police. By

now, Azeem has stopped fighting. It wasn't doing him any good anyway. He looks wilted, done. They take us out the front door. I see Ms. Singh push the principal out of the way so she can stick right with us. I am terrified.

Outside there are police cars and vans, and more officers with guns drawn. A television truck is there. I think about being on *Reach for the Top*, a crazy thing to think about.

"What's this?" a man in authority asks. I know he's in authority because of the white shirt and tie. "Who's this kid?" He's pointing at me.

"There were two Arab kids in the room. We weren't sure, so we brought them both."

"I'm Haroon Badawi. I'm Persian," I say. Actually, I'm third-generation Canadian. I don't know why I think they should know where my ancestors came from.

"Did he resist? Assault you? Do anything we can bring him in for?"

"He absolutely did not!" Ms. Singh charges in. "Neither boy did. Release them both now!"

"He could be in on it," the cop holding me says. "I say take them both in to be safe."

"Uncuff him," the man with the tie says. "I'll be the one hauled up on wrongful arrest, not you." He turns to me. "This is your lucky day. Don't make us regret it. No hard feelings, eh?" He picks up my

23

hand and shakes it, turning us a little so the television camera has a clear view. "Put him in the car," he says to the officer holding Azeem.

Azeem is folded into the back seat of a police car, one cop keeping his hand on the top of Azeem's head so it doesn't bang on the doorframe. The door is closed on him. I see his face looking out at me through the window, his body in an uncomfortable posture, his hands bound behind him.

I feel that I should say something. He's my teammate, after all. But I don't even wave as he is driven away.

"Take Haroon back to the classroom and wait for the all clear," the principal says to Ms. Singh. "We will talk later about your breach of discipline."

"I'll call my union," Ms. Singh replies. "They love talking about discipline." She puts her hand around my arm in case the police change their minds and make a grab for me again.

We walk again past the faces pressed against the classroom windows. We walk by police searching lockers and holding onto dogs. We move as quickly as we can back to the world of *Reach for the Top*.

I really start to cry when the classroom door closes, all the fear catching up to me. Someone offers me a tissue, and I try to stop shaking.

"Theme round," Ms. Singh says. "The subject is police brutality."

Is it possible to know too much about a subject? Nadia's brothers and father were massacred in Kosovo. Nygen's parents were boat people. Marie comes from Haiti, José from El Salvador. I am two generations removed from my grandparents' troubles in Herat, and we are all here now in this land of peace and safety. But suddenly it feels like we never left home.

We are in lockdown for another hour. We don't drill. We just talk. We bump our stories up against each other until our little classroom seems to contain the whole history of the world. Then Ms. Singh teaches us a song she learned on a desert trek in Morocco, about a camel that's smarter than its owner. We sing it very loud. I get the feeling she hopes the police or our principal will be annoyed.

The principal's voice comes over the PA again. "The lockdown is over. All students are to leave the school property immediately. Do not go to your lockers! Leave the school immediately!"

We all get slowly to our feet. None of us is anxious to leave our little cocoon. Outside there will be questions, rumors. Jerks.

"We know that Azeem has a good mind, a good heart, and a good sense of humor," Ms. Singh says. "Whatever they are accusing him of, we know these three things to be true."

It's a good way to end a very strange afternoon.

25

She opens the door, and we join the river of students.

I don't take ten steps before I hear the words. *Terrorists. Suicide bombers.*

Twenty-four-hour news coverage and cell phones have had parents calling kids and kids calling each other.

The hallways, usually full of talk about dating, sports, music, and teachers are now full of talk about bombs, terror cells, Al Qaeda, and the police. The police are still here, but not as many. They are hustling kids out of the school.

I feel something grab my arm. I turn and look into the face of a Rasta ventriloquist's dummy— dreadlocks and eyes and a smile. It's wearing a clerical collar.

"You apologized nicely, so they let you go?"

The puppet is carried by Julian, my best friend. He's practicing to be a ventriloquist. He made the puppet in his own image—all hair and cool. Julian's not wearing preacher's clothes, though. He's wearing a t-shirt with a big yellow smiley face on it.

"What's with the collar?" I ask.

"I'm trying out a different character. Meet Reverend Bob." Julian makes the dummy bow its head and say, "Bless you, my son." In his normal voice, he says, "I'm getting better, don't you think?"

"I saw your ears move," I say.

"So what happened?"

"Mistaken identity," I say. Later, away from the crowds, I'll tell him the whole story.

"There are rumors bouncing off the walls," he says.

"Hey! Look at me! I'm Osama bin Laden!" A group of little white ninth graders are horsing around. One wraps his gym shirt around his head, yammers a lot of gibberish, tossing in the words "Allah be praised," and ending up with "I command you to blow up the world!"

I start to turn away, but Julian grabs the kid and yanks the shirt away. "You trying to start a riot?" he asks. "Go home. Don't be so stupid." The grade niners badmouth us, but they leave. We're taller and they don't know me well enough to figure out that I'm no fighter.

"Things are going to get crazy!" Reverend Bob says in a thick Jamaican accent.

I agree with the good reverend. He, Julian, and I make our way out of the school. The front is still littered with police cars and media. Some television people are interviewing students. We keep our heads down and walk away quickly.

CHAPTER THREE

JAY

THE CAR SQUEALED as Kevin pulled away. "I can't believe they canceled football practice!" he said angrily.

"You better slow down," I warned him. There were still some police cars around.

"They're not interested in me," he said. "They've got other things on their minds."

I guess he was right about that. We were still confused about what had happened. But obviously it had to be serious, because you don't bring in SWAT teams to issue traffic tickets. Something bad had happened, and football had to take a back seat.

Kevin didn't like anything getting in the way of football. For him, football was the most important thing about school—probably the most important thing, period. Besides being captain, he was the best player on the team. He was a guaranteed prospect for university ball, and it wasn't unusual for two or three college scouts to be in the bleachers at our games, watching and drooling over him.

The scouts' interest in Kevin didn't hurt the rest of us either. Those scouts didn't just see him play. Up until this year, I'd never even considered that I might also be a prospect for college ball. I'd just never thought about it.

Sure, I'd been a star player in my little country school playing against other little country schools. But this was different. This was a big school in a big city, and here I was starting on that team. Now I was seriously thinking about college ball.

Kevin squealed around the corner, cutting off another car. The other driver honked and Kevin put his hand out the window and gestured at him. Kevin was never timid behind the wheel, so being ticked off about practice wasn't about to make him any less aggressive.

I didn't care about practice. I was just glad to be out of the building. For the better part of two hours, we'd sat in the dark—in more ways than one. After a while, Steve had started to call some friends on his cell, trying to piece together what was happening in other parts of the building. Everybody seemed to know a little. But nobody had heard anything about a brawl or a drug bust. The only weapons anybody had seen had belonged to the cops. But why so many cops and so many weapons, and why the bomb squad? Had there been a bomb? What could that kid have possibly done?

We'd learned that it was not just the exits we'd seen but every exit in the school had been blocked off

29

by the police. Nobody had been allowed to leave until they'd been checked. At the same time, the special cops had searched the school, looking for specific people. As far as anybody had known, only one of the students had been arrested.

We didn't know him. Somebody had mentioned a name to Steve, but it was really strange sounding, and now I couldn't even remember it. Just something foreign and funny sounding.

We knew who might be brawling or selling drugs. Everybody in the school knew the names of the dealers, but the guy who was arrested was practically a stranger, right off the radar.

That wasn't so surprising. He was brown. Not black—Steve was half black, and a bunch of our teammates were black.

The brown kids were from India or Pakistan or some place in the Middle East. Back in my old school there was only one brown kid. His parents ran the gas station on the edge of town. He was a grade down from me, and although his name was Ali, he insisted that everybody call him Al. He seemed like a pretty good guy. Here at this school, there were lots of brown people. My math class was more brown than white.

The brown kids seemed to spend a lot of time in the library, and they sat at their own tables in the corner of the cafeteria.

The cafeteria had lots of different sections. The jocks, guys like us, sat right by the cash registers, where we could get food fast as well as check out everybody going through the lines.

Up by the stage, as close as they could get without actually being on the stage, sat the preppy, pretty, popular girls. They liked to be seen, and that worked out well because basically they *were* being looked at all the time. We jocks didn't dress preppy, but we went to the same parties as them. Most of the cheerleaders came from those tables.

Over by the side doors, almost out of the cafeteria, were the Goths and emos. The Goths were all dressed in identical black clothes and makeup to show what individuals they were. The emos were sort of diet-Goth or Goth light. They wore less makeup and fewer accessories, like studs and such. They all listened to sad, solemn, deep music. Most of them looked like they were going to break into tears at any moment. If you said "Boo!" they might jump, scatter like birds, or wet themselves—or all of the above. There were only two or three of them in my old school. Here, they formed their own little cheering— or crying—section.

Then there was Cafrica, the section where the black kids sat. Some of the jocks sat with us, but most of them just clustered together in a self-segregated group. Martin Luther King may have had a dream,

31

but at this school, the kids were wide-awake and wide apart.

Hilariously, just over from them sat a bunch of brown and Asian kids who wore bandanas, backward baseball caps, and basketball jerseys—even though they didn't play ball. They were sort of pretending they were black. I'd heard the other Chinese kids call them Blackie Chans.

Sometimes it seemed like there were as many subgroups as there were tables. In my old school, there had been divisions, but not nearly as many as here. And they had nothing to do with race or religion.

In this school, there were lots and lots of East Indian or Middle Eastern or whatever kids—the brown kids. They even had their own place where they sat just outside the building, in a corner of the school property. We called it Brown Town. *They* called it Brown Town. I didn't really know any of them. Hardly any of them ever tried out for school teams. Too busy studying, I guess.

When the PA finally signaled the all clear, we were told to leave the school by the nearest exit, without going to our lockers. That was it, the whole message, no explanation. Nothing, just get out of the school.

— ✳ —

"You know we can't afford to miss any practices," Kevin said.

I knew I was going to hear about it the whole ride home.

"We didn't play well last game," he added.

"We won by twenty-two points."

"I *know* how much we won by," he snapped. "What I'm saying is, we didn't play well. A captain's job is to demand the best from everybody, every game. You have to learn that."

I had lots to learn. I was just a junior and relatively new to the school. I wasn't even an assistant captain—that honor was reserved for seniors. But I also knew what was happening. It was a tradition at our school. Every year, the coaches, captain, and assistants selected one grade-eleven player. It was somebody who was a starter, somebody they thought could be a leader, somebody who would be the captain the following year. That was me.

Ever since football season started, I had been spending more of my time with Kevin and the assistant captains than the friends from my own year. It was different hanging out with the really cool football-jock seniors. And it wasn't just during school time. I went to all the best parties, the ones that those preppy popular senior *girls* went to. Suddenly, girls who last spring hadn't even noticed me as I walked down the halls turned and said hello and were all friendly. Football was a good thing, and being Kevin's friend was even better.

33

Kevin always drove me home after practice. He had the coolest car in the school—including the teachers. It was a dark blue BMW with a killer sound system and a six-speed stick. Kevin was rich...well, his family was rich.

We pulled over to the curb in front of my house and I climbed out.

"You need a ride tomorrow?" he asked.

"My mother said she can drive me. Are you sure morning practice is still on?"

"It'd *better* be on. See you at seven."

"Later," I said. I pushed the door closed and he roared away.

I looked at my watch. It was just past 3:30. No homework—all my books were trapped in my locker, and we'd been ordered to leave without going to our lockers. I had a free evening. It felt like a gift.

"I'm home!" I yelled as I started to kick off my shoes.

"Jay!" my mother exclaimed. She rushed out of the living room, wrapped her arms around me, and gave me a big hug and held on.

"Thank goodness you're okay," she said as she released her grip and looked up at me.

"Why wouldn't I be okay?"

"The news. It's all over the news. I can't believe it—a terrorist at your school."

"What?" I gasped.

"A terrorist. He was a student at your school."

"Come on," I said, shaking my head in disbelief. "Get serious. There was no terrorist. It was just a kid…a kid from my school."

"A kid who was *part* of a group of terrorists. The authorities have arrested seventeen people across the whole city. They were members of terrorist cells that planned to blow up schools, government buildings, and the subway! It's all over the news."

She gestured to the living room, where the TV was on.

"I have to call your father and let him know that you're home safe."

She rushed away. Stunned, I stepped toward the TV but stopped as I realized I still had one shoe on. I kicked it off, went into the living room, and sat on the couch. The TV was blaring, and the picture on the all-news channel showed a reporter standing directly in front of our school's main entrance. Across the bottom of the screen in large letters was a banner that read LIVE.

Before I could even catch any of what he was saying, the scene shifted. It was another reporter, standing in front of what looked like an office building. Behind him were dozens of regular police officers and those special cops with helmets. Some were carrying shields. Marching between the two columns of police were five, six, or maybe more men. Their hands were cuffed and their heads were covered so they couldn't be identified. Was one of them the guy from my school?

"We are watching," the announcer said, "the arrival of some of the suspects who were arrested today in a massive operation that involved over three hundred officers from three separate levels of government. In a series of simultaneous raids across the country, police arrested suspects in alleged terrorist cells."

I grabbed the remote and turned the volume up even louder.

"While information is still limited in this breaking story, we can report that police sources have indicated that thus far sixteen adults and one juvenile have been arrested."

Juvenile. The kid from my school.

"While police have not confirmed or denied that more suspects are being sought, it is believed that more arrests are imminent and—" The reporter stopped mid-sentence and put his hand against his ear. I figured he was getting a message in his earpiece.

"We now go live to police headquarters for an announcement."

Once more, the picture changed. There was an empty podium with about half a dozen microphones attached. Reporters with cameras and more microphones huddled in front, shuffling for position.

Three men in police uniform came up to the front, and one stepped up to the podium. He pulled a piece of paper from his breast pocket, unfolded it, and straightened it out on the podium.

"Good afternoon, ladies and gentlemen," he said. He sounded nervous, and his voice cracked over the last word.

Underneath his picture a graphic banner appeared, identifying him as Police Chief Timothy Brown.

"I will read from a prepared statement," he said, his head down. "Today, our force, assisted by federal forces, initiated a series of fully coordinated raids designed to arrest members of four terrorist cells. There were seventeen people arrested. They have been under surveillance for the past six months, and their intent and actions have been closely monitored. This morning we arrested two suspects who allegedly attempted to purchase a quantity of ammonium nitrate, a fertilizer which can be used to make bombs."

"Oh, my goodness." It was my mother. She was standing right behind me. "That's what they used to destroy that building in Oklahoma."

I shushed her. I wanted to hear the rest.

"Along with attempting to purchase the material needed to make bombs, one suspect was also carrying a list of schools, subway lines, and government buildings where we believe these bombs were to be carried, or placed, and detonated.

"In addition, these suspects were engaged in recruiting and training more terrorists at a remote wooded area north of the city."

The chief paused and took a sip from a glass sitting on the side of the podium. He looked nervous, but who could blame him?

"All of the suspects are citizens, either born in this country, with landed immigrant status or recently obtained citizenship. While these are allegedly home-grown terrorist cells, we have reason to believe that they are connected with international terrorist organizations, including Al Qaeda."

"Wow," I said. It was more like a gasp. That was just crazy. No way could a kid at our school be part of any terrorist cell, and certainly not one connected to Osama bin Laden. Is that why there were so many cops at the school—did they think he was hiding in the cafeteria?

"Through internet connections, in chat rooms, and through telephone conversations that have been traced, monitored, or recorded, authorities were able to piece together the conspiracy," the chief said. "In fact, when the suspects purchased what they thought was ammonium nitrate, the fertilizer had been replaced by a harmless substance. The public was never at risk."

That was slick. You had to give them credit for being smart.

"Due to the ongoing nature of the investigation and the extreme sensitivity and scope of the operation, further information will not be given at this time in order not to jeopardize ongoing investigation or compromise the rights of the accused to a fair hearing in court." He looked up. "I will not be taking any questions at this time. Thank you."

He walked away from the podium and he was bathed in the flashes of a hundred different cameras. The picture cut back to one of the reporters, the one standing in front of the big building.

"To recap," he said. "In what is becoming the largest story of the day internationally, police have made arrests in a conspiracy involving seventeen people who are alleged to be part of a conspiracy with ties to Al Qaeda. It has now been confirmed that in addition to attempting to purchase material to make bombs, specific government and public locations were identified by the group as potential targets."

"Your father takes the subway every day."

"I can't believe anybody would bomb our subways."

"Why not? They bombed trains in Spain and subways in London. Why not here?" she asked.

That thought jarred me. I didn't have an answer... why not here?

"Look, there's your school again," Mom said, pointing at the screen.

There was a scene—obviously pre-taped—show-ing all the police cars, the lights flashing, parked everywhere—on the pavement, on the sidewalk, even up on the grass by the football field. I clearly recognized the scene. It was a different angle of what I'd seen from the roof.

"One of the alleged offenders arrested," the announcer said, "is a student at Central Secondary School."

The picture switched to the two students being led out of the school in handcuffs. The camera peered through the officers at the two suspects. One was facing away but the other looked almost right at the camera. He looked familiar...I thought. He was maybe a year older than me, a senior. Brown skin, a little growth of hair on his upper lip and cheeks, dark, dark eyes that looked angry.

The camera angle was blocked by one of the offi-cers and then it snaked around and the second sus-pect turned around—I couldn't believe it.

"I know that kid," I gasped.

"You do?"

"He's in my geography class...he sits up front at the side. His name is..." I struggled to come up with it. I knew it was something funny...it started with an H... "Haroon. His name is Haroon."

"I can't believe you had a terrorist in your class."

"I can't believe *that* kid is a terrorist. He just sits

there, taking notes. He doesn't even answer questions. He's the quietest kid in the class."

"Isn't that what you always hear when they interview the neighbors of murderers—*he was so quiet, he kept to himself.*"

Actually, that *was* what they did always say.

"I just can't believe there was a terrorist a few seats away from you."

"There wasn't. They let him go," I said, "so obviously he wasn't a terrorist—it was just mistaken identity…a lot of those brown kids look the same to me."

The screen changed to an inside shot of the school. Two police officers leading a dog down the deserted hall. This had to be after the lockdown was ordered.

"Police brought in both dogs and the bomb disposal robot," the announcer said.

"There was a bomb at the school?" my mother questioned anxiously.

There was now footage of a strange little mechanical robot rolling jerkily down one of the hallways… it was by the shop classes. That made sense. Most of the brown kids chose to have their lockers in that corridor.

"The remote vehicle," the announcer continued, "was used to open and examine the contents of the locker belonging to the alleged suspect. Unofficial sources claim that there were no explosives or toxic materials discovered in the school."

"Thank goodness," my mother said.

"They obviously didn't check out the chili surprise in the cafeteria," I said.

"How can you joke about something like this?" my mother asked.

I shook my head. "I guess because none of it seems real. I just can't believe that some kid from my school could be part of a terrorist plot."

"If the police say he is, he is."

"Haven't you ever heard of innocent until proven guilty?" I asked, parroting something from my law class.

"Don't you think the police would be one hundred percent certain before they made these arrests?" she asked. "Didn't you hear what the police chief said? They have all sorts of proof. The police don't arrest innocent people."

"Ever?" I questioned.

"Not in a case like this," she said, shaking her head. "Thank goodness for our police forces. It sounds like they stopped something terrible before it happened."

Without her saying another word, I knew what she was thinking about. Everybody had seen the pictures on TV. Subways, trains, the Twin Towers. London, Spain, New York.

"I think we can all breathe a little easier now."

"I don't know about that," I said.

She gave me a questioning look.

"Didn't *you* hear what he said about there being an ongoing investigation? Maybe they're going to be arresting other people. Maybe even at my school."

My mother looked genuinely worried.

I didn't believe that. I just liked making her worried.

"Do you really think there are more terrorists at your school?"

I laughed. "I told you, I can't believe there are *any* terrorists at my school."

"Nothing like this ever happened at your old school."

"That's because *nothing* ever happened at my old school." It was so much smaller, and everything moved slower.

"Thank goodness you've found such nice friends here, at least," she said.

"It was close there for a while," I said. "I wasn't sure whether I should hang out with the guys on the football team or the terrorists."

"You shouldn't joke about something like that."

"Okay, I'll get serious. I'm seriously hungry. Is it possible for me to get a little snack before supper?"

"That can be arranged." She bent down and gave me a kiss on the forehead. I was getting a little old for that...at least, if somebody was around to see it.

My mother went into the kitchen to make me something and I turned my attention back to the news.

CHAPTER FOUR

HAROON

MY FATHER IS MAKING his famous lamb casserole for supper. It's famous in his own mind but in no one else's.

"I hope you worked up an appetite," he says when I walk in. Then he looks up at the clock. "You're early. Did you get expelled?"

He makes jokes like that because he knows that getting expelled, or even suspended, is the least likely thing to happen to me.

My father doesn't listen to the radio except for concerts on the public stations. He says the music helps him concentrate on his writing. He pays as little attention to the modern news as he possibly can. If it didn't happen at least two hundred years ago, he's not interested. He wouldn't have heard anything about my day.

"No, but I almost got arrested."

"Did you?" he says, without looking up. "That seems to happen all the time."

"I'm serious. I almost got arrested."

That gets his attention. He nods at the celery on

the chopping board. I wash my hands and get busy.

"It will probably be on the news tonight," I say, wishing I didn't have to tell him. "There were TV cameras there."

"TV cameras?" he repeats. I can't read the expression on his face. It's deeper than the usual parental concern. "This was something big, then." He keeps his voice calm, though.

I take after him, most of the time. I keep my voice calm too. "We were put on lockdown," I say, and then I tell him the whole story, seeing the anger flash on his face when I mention the handcuffs. I get almost to the end when Zana bounces into the house, her basketball bouncing at the same time. She gets a frown from my father, but it's tempered with a wink and a kiss. She puts the ball down anyway and starts munching on the celery I've cleaned and chopped.

"Did he tell you?" she asks.

"You interrupted me," I say.

"Did he tell you that kids are saying he turned the other student over to the police so he could take his spot on the *Reach for the Top* team?"

That stops me. My father stops performing his so-called magic with the spices.

I don't know what to say. I want to say it's not true, but the idea of defending myself to my family is absurd.

"Rumors blow over," my father says.

45

"I don't think this one will," Zana says. I try to hand her a knife. If she's going to eat, she can help chop. She ignores it. "It might get overshadowed, though. I stopped at Sarah's house to watch the news. *They* have cable," she adds, as a dig at my father. "The police arrested seventeen people, including Azeem. They say they've uncovered a plot to blow up other high schools, government buildings, the subway.

"This is serious. They're saying he did all these terrible things, that he belongs to an international terror network."

"He's *seventeen*," I say.

"His poor parents," my father says. He perfects the seasoning and scoops up the celery before Zana can eat it all. "All the families must be scared."

"Could they send him to Guantánamo?"

My head snaps up when I hear Zana ask that question. My mind sees images of blindfolded men in cages, guarded by soldiers. I can't picture Azeem there. I refuse to. Azeem belongs on the *Reach for the Top* team. Until this moment, I haven't really grasped what is going on.

"He's a kid," I say. "There are rules and laws. Procedures." I took law in grade ten.

"Climb down off your dream cloud," Zana says. "Other kids have been sent there. They're still there." She sticks her head in the fridge. My father steers her toward a bowl of apples on the kitchen counter.

"Lamb casserole?" She turns to me and makes a face. "Your turn to pay for the pizza."

Dad acts offended but we know he's not. He grabs us and holds us close. I know he's thinking about the parents who cannot hold their children today, who cannot present them with plates of food and watch them eat and argue and laugh. I know he's thinking that because I am thinking the same thing. And so is Zana.

Later we manage to eat the lamb casserole without keeling over. Dad puts a portion away for Mom when she gets home from the hospital. She specializes in high-risk pregnancies, so her schedule isn't regular. If there is a new mother in trouble, she hates to leave at the end of her shift. Dad's hours at the university are more regular.

All through dinner, Zana talks about the arrests. "How will you defend yourself?" she asks me.

"Defend myself against what?"

"Against that rumor. Kids will want to know why they let you go."

"Don't defend yourself," Dad says. "Only a fool defends himself against foolishness."

"Is that a quote from Dickens?" I help myself to more casserole. It's not half bad this time.

"It's a quote from me," Dad says. "You're in high school, a hotbed of hormonal drama. By tomorrow, it will be forgotten."

Zana starts to argue, but she is easily distracted by a discussion over whose turn it is to do the dishes. It's hers, which she knows full well. But she argues the point anyway, to see if she can wear me down. She can't. Not tonight.

Later, we watch the local news on one of the two television channels we can get without cable. The arrests take up most of the broadcasts. Police Chief Timothy Brown's face fills the screen, talking about the extraordinary cooperation between many agencies in thwarting this terrible threat to our way of life.

"I want to assure the public that safety is uppermost in all of our minds. It's important that we go about our daily lives as usual. To do otherwise would let the terrorists win. But we welcome the public's cooperation in reporting anything suspicious to the police."

"Live your life but watch your neighbors," says Zana. "What's suspicious? Muslims. We're suspicious. Islamic terrorists, they said. The men who blew up that building in Oklahoma City were Christians, but no one called them Christian terrorists."

"Quiet," I say. Zana tosses a cushion at my head but stops talking for now. The police chief is saying that these arrests in no way reflect badly on the Islamic community as a whole. The camera pulls back and shows him shaking hands with a group of Islamic leaders. "There's our imam," I say.

One by one, the leaders call for peace and reason.

"They couldn't find one woman?" Zana grumbles. All the leaders standing with the chief are men.

"Go down there and tell them off," I say. "Give us some peace." I knock her feet off the footstool to make room for my own.

In the last few months, my feet and arms and torso have finally caught up with each other. For the longest time I was tripping over rugs and knocking over lamps because I was growing so quickly and, it seemed, unevenly. Even though I'm finally taller than Zana, she can still beat me in basketball.

"You don't care about anything as long as you have your quiet little life," she says, snatching the footstool back. I let her have it. We're getting too big to wrestle. Besides, she's better coordinated than I am.

"I don't get much of a chance for a quiet life with you around," I say.

"Well, I don't like quiet. I like action," Zana says, jumping around in her chair. Zana rarely keeps still.

"Go blow something up, then," I say. "Go form the Islamic Women's Liberation Front, blow up symbols of oppression, and leave me alone."

"The first thing we'll blow up is you," Zana says. It's a normal exchange for us, done without rancor.

"No one is blowing anyone up," our father says automatically. His attention is divided by the old English law book he's reading.

49

Zana won't let it go. "I wonder what they're say-ing about you in the chat rooms."

"About me?" Our father raises his head, per-plexed.

"About Haroon."

Dad goes back to his book. "I'm sure they're say-ing he's a handsome boy who does his turn at the dishes without arguing." Zana tosses a cushion at his head in response. Dad laughs and tosses it back.

The story winds down with more footage of our school. The very last shot is of the police officer shak-ing hands with me and smiling.

Zana shuts off the TV—she has to do it manually because we don't have a remote—then she turns and hovers over me with her hands on her hips.

"You shook their hands? They just hauled a Muslim kid off to jail, and you shake their hands?"

"It was one hand, and I didn't shake his, he shook mine. I didn't exactly have a choice." I try to push her away, but she's like a vulture, waiting for some-thing to die.

"Didn't have a choice? You couldn't put your hands behind your back?"

"It happened too fast," I say, but there's a doubt now in my mind. It makes me feel worse. "They had only just uncuffed me," I add, but that sounds like pleading.

"You know how this looks, don't you? How am I

going to explain this to my friends?" Zana leaves me and stomps outside. Moments later, I hear the basketball bouncing. She uses basketball to take the edge off her temper. Sometimes it works.

I look for help from Dad, some word of reassurance, but he's buried in his book. Oddly, I do find that reassuring. Zana's outburst and my police handshake aren't important enough for him to return to this century.

It's a funny feeling having no homework. I sit down at my computer, thinking about what Zana said. Would they be talking about me? I bend down to turn it on, then sit up again. I don't really want to know.

I picked up the Dickens habit from Dad. The easiest way to make modern problems disappear is to slip into the pages of *Oliver Twist* or *Bleak House*. I stretch out on my bed and read. I fall asleep with a workhouse full of orphans spread across my chest.

I wake up when Mom knocks and comes into my room. She sits down on the side of my bed.

"Good day?" I ask, my head still full of sleep.

"A good day," she replies.

That's sort of a family code we've developed. A good day means she didn't lose any of the moms or babies in her care. If it's a bad day, sometimes she doesn't feel like talking about it. It's shorthand. If she comes home in a bad mood, we know why, and give her time to get out of it.

"What about you?" she asks.

"A strange day." I rub my eyes.

"I saw the news. And your father called me. Are you all right?"

"It doesn't seem real."

"Maybe it isn't," she says. "Maybe by tomorrow it will have all blown over." She gives me a kiss and says goodnight. "Just remember that you are an honorable young man and have nothing to be ashamed of." She leaves my room to get her supper.

I look at the room I've grown up in. It's nothing fancy. We aren't fancy people. We believe in reading books, serving others, and being together. But the furniture is solid, the rugs and curtains thick. I keep a tidy room because that's how I like it. The few bits of boyhood still here—a shelf of model ships I built, a few shells I picked up on our camping trip to Nantucket when I was nine—blend in neatly with the dictionary, computer, and the poster of the periodic table. (I'm hoping the information on the poster will seep into my brain as I sleep. Chemistry is a struggle.)

Bits of Afghanistan are here and there too—little touches of old family belongings that managed to survive time and distance. I feel rooted in this room, to my family, and to the values that hold us together.

Outside my room, I can hear Zana arguing with Mom about some little thing. I can't decipher the words, but I can tell from the tone that it's a good-natured argument. Perhaps she's given up her militancy already. Zana gets crazy notions in her head and holds onto them as if they were a universal truth. But then another more appealing idea comes along, and she embraces that one just as strongly. We're twins, but we're not very much alike.

My room is normal, my mother and sister having an argument is normal, my father getting lost in his research is normal. My house and my world are solid around me.

High school is always crazy, I remind myself. Tomorrow there will be a whole new craziness.

I put out my light. I don't remember getting much sleep.

— ✳ —

There are police cars outside our school again the next morning, although not as many. Just two or three. I ignore them. I'm looking for Julian. He'll have something sane to say about the whole mess.

I spy him and Reverend Bob in Brown Town. We didn't give the area that name. The white kids started calling it that and it stuck. Some of us even call it that now, even though it's insulting. Muslims come in all colors. But it's just easier to say, "Meet you in Brown Town" than "Meet you on that patch of grass outside the home economics room on the northeast corner of the school."

Julian is Jamaican—or his parents are. He was born here, and they're all citizens now. He doesn't really belong in Brown Town, but things like that don't bother Julian. Any group of people is an audience. He goes where he wants, and he gets away with it too.

I wave, and he makes the Reverend Bob wave back. I start to cross the quad to meet him.

"It's Haroon, isn't it?"

A man in a suit comes out of nowhere and stands in front of me. He holds out a police badge.

"Yes," I say. "My name is Haroon." I try to keep walking, but the officer puts his hand on my arm. He doesn't grab it, but I sure know it's there.

"What's your hurry? School bell won't ring for twenty minutes." He holds out his hand for me to shake. "I'm Detective Kenneth Moffett. Just wanted to tell you again how sorry we all are about yesterday. Mistaking you for a terrorist, I mean. Mistakes happen. We hope you won't hold it against us."

He is standing close and speaking quietly. I see all sorts of faces turned our way.

"Someone apologized yesterday," I say. "I have to go."

"You don't mind if we chat for a moment, do you?" With his arm around my shoulder, Detective Moffett walks me to the police car at the curb. Another officer is standing by the car and opens the back door. "Slide on in there for a moment."

"We can talk out here," I say, knowing how many eyes are on us—on me. The police are not supposed to question a minor without a parent present, I remember from law class. I'm about to assert my rights, but then I start to wonder if I'm remembering it correctly. Instead, all I manage is a feeble "I really have nothing to say."

"Get in the car, Haroon, unless you want us to think you've got something to hide."

It doesn't feel like I have a choice. I get in. They close the door. I've never been in the back of a police car before. I look at the door and realize there's no way to get out from the inside. I start to shake. I hope I hide it well.

Two cops get into the front seat and a third gets into the back with me. They all turn and look at me. For a long time, no one says anything. Then the officer in the driver's seat says to me, "It's a heck of a thing we've got here."

"A heck of a thing," the man next to him says.

"We're talking about serious threats on the lives of a lot of people," Detective Moffett says. "Did you ever stop to think about what blowing up a school would do—not just to our city, but to our whole country? Did you?"

I shake my head.

"People would become too afraid to let their children go to school. The education system would collapse. The economic fallout would be staggering. An attack on a school is an attack on our entire way of life. Now, just imagine if the subway system or our government buildings were no longer safe either. Imagine what *that* would do to the economy."

Ms. Singh would have a field day with that sort of logic. I imagine her now, leaping around with her quick feet and her quick mind. In my nervousness, I find the image funny, and my lips twitch. I bite them, to make them stop.

"I'm glad that amuses you," the officer in the front passenger seat says. "I think he's in on it," he says to the driver. "I think we should question him at the station." He switches back to me. "You laugh at treason?"

Treason is a word that takes the twitch out of my lips and makes me go cold. It's a word out of history, a word with beheadings.

"Oh, that may not be the legal definition of treason," he continues, "but that's what it amounts to. A traitor to our way of life."

Another long silence. I try to pretend I'm James Bond, cool and with a bag of tricks up my sleeve. It's not working.

"Don't be afraid, Haroon," Detective Moffett says with a quick glare at the cops in the front. "We know you weren't involved. You come from a good, respectable family. Father a professor. Mother a doctor. Your family has tried hard to fit in. Not like some of these others."

My brain is racing as fast as my pulse. How do they know about my family? And do they think they compliment me by insulting others?

But I'm too scared to defend myself or anybody else.

"It must have been a shock to see your friend taken away like that," the officer on the other side of me says.

"Azeem's not my friend. We're not even in the same grade," I say. Immediately I want to snatch the words back. It's true that we're not friends, not like me and Julian. But we do the *Reach for the Top* thing, and we have fun doing that. I want to explain, but I feel thick and stupid.

"Maybe you have some sense after all, Haroon," the police officer in the driver's seat says. "Friends like that are dangerous to keep. Your whole future could go down the tubes, with friends like that."

I run my hand along the armrest on the door, hoping they don't notice, hoping to find a secret button that will spring the door open.

"I'm sure your family is proud of you," says Detective Moffett. "You're not going to get mixed up with bombings. And you know that withholding information from the police about these things is just as bad as doing them yourself. Worse, even, because you know it's wrong. You're not all full of these crazy notions that are damaging the good name of your religion around the world. What is that saying? 'All it takes for evil to triumph is for men of goodwill to do nothing.'"

They stare at me, hard. I don't want to look at them, and I don't want to look away. Detective Moffett gives me his card. "Call me about anything day or night. Let's clear up this mess."

I take the card. I don't have the guts to refuse it. "I don't know anything," I say. There's no way to say that without sounding guilty.

"A lot of people think they don't know anything. But then, when they really start to think about it, they realize they know more than they thought."

Then they all start to ask questions, rapid-fire, like Ms. Singh during a drill. One right after the other.

"Do you think you might be one of those people?"

"Do you think you might know something? And if you do, will you share what you know, or will you keep it to yourself?"

"Will your parents continue to be proud of you, or will they be sitting on a cold, hard bench outside the courtroom, weeping and wondering what happened to their cute little boy?"

"Will you help us or will you help them? There's no middle ground. We are in a war. In a war, there are no innocent bystanders."

"A rabbi, a priest, and a police captain walk into a donut shop," says a voice.

There's a knock at the window beside me. I turn my head and there's the grinning puppet face of Reverend Bob, joined a second later by the grinning face of Julian. He makes Reverend Bob tap on the front window.

"Can Haroon come out and play?"

Amazingly, they let me go. They open my door and I don't look back. Julian puts his arm around my shoulder and walks me though the jungle of staring faces. He and Reverend Bob engage in wild conversation, giving me cover until we get through the school doors and go our separate ways to class.

CHAPTER FIVE

JAY

I DOUBLED OVER, partly to catch my breath and partly to reduce the stitch in my side. Please, not another wind sprint. Not another punishment run. The coaches kept yelling at us to stop talking and focus. We were focused. Just not on football.

I've never liked football practice, and this one was particularly brutal. But this morning I didn't mind. It was as brutal as usual, but it was also familiar and normal. The sun was bright, with a few clouds in the sky and a gentle breeze. It seemed as if we owned the place, especially for the first hour when the school was practically deserted. Maybe you could find a teacher or two, the principal, some kids at band practice, but practically nobody.

And then, like a dam busting, the parking lot was filled with cars and trucks and motorcycles. Music blared, engines roared, and horns went off as people jockeyed for parking spots, dropped off kids, or just tried to attract attention. Maybe they just needed to hear themselves—*I honk, therefore I am.*

As usual, some groups of students wandered

over to sit in the bleachers or stand along the side-lines. We had an audience. And despite how tired we were from the first hour of the practice, we all dug a little deeper, ran a little faster, and hit a little harder.

I play football, therefore I am.

I surveyed the whole scene. Despite the chaos, it all seemed calm. Everything was happening the way it was supposed to happen. There were no police cars ringing the school. No news trucks beaming up satellite feeds. No bomb-sniffing dogs or robots looking for explosives. Or students in handcuffs.

I still couldn't believe that it had been real. It was as if I'd watched a TV drama the day before, not real news about our school, about our community.

"Everybody, bring it in!" our head coach Mr. Pruit yelled, his voice cracking over the last two words.

We all trotted over and gathered around him and the other coaches. Some of the players slumped to the ground and others stood, forming a big circle. I always stood, along with Kevin and the assistant captains. I wanted to take off my helmet to cool down. But Kevin kept his helmet on, so I did too.

Nobody spoke. All eyes were on Coach. We all knew that if even one person talked or wasn't paying attention that we'd all have to do a lap of the track. That was the price of building team unity.

"I'd like to tell all of you what happened here at the school yesterday," he said.

Now nobody needed to fake paying attention.

"But unfortunately," Mr. Pruit continued, "I don't know. Nobody knows. All the information we have is the same thing you heard on the news or read in the papers this morning."

It had been front page of the paper this morning—the entire front page. Big bold headlines over top of a picture of a group of men, their heads covered, in cuffs, being led away. There was even a little article in the bottom corner with the heading High School Terrorist. It mentioned our school by name as well as the locations of the other arrests.

Usually we only got mentioned after a football game, and that was on the last page of the sports section under the High School Sports listing. That's where I usually started reading. Not the High School Sports listing, but the sports section. This morning I'd run out and got the paper off the porch and I was so busy reading the first section, I hadn't even gotten to sports or comics.

"Who read the paper this morning?" Coach asked.

Most hands went up.

"So you know as much about what happened at the school as I do. A kid—I don't even know who he is except by name. I never coached the boy or taught him history—has been charged with being part of a group that was going to bomb some buildings or such. That's all I know."

A hand shot up and Coach motioned for him to speak.

"Will they tell us more today in school? You know, make some sort of announcement?"

Coach shook his head. "I don't think administration knows much, and even if the school did know, they couldn't tell anybody. Privacy issues, especially when it involves minors. We're running out of time, so I do want to talk to you about something pretty important." He paused and his face got all serious. I tried to figure out what it could be.

"All you boys who read the paper this morning, can any one of you tell me what place our team is ranked?"

That's right, it was Tuesday, the day the rankings came out listing every football team. I'd forgotten to even look.

A few hands went up, including Kevin's. He was standing right beside me.

"Kevin," Coach said.

"We're ranked fifth."

Fifth. I couldn't believe it. We had been third the week before, but then we went on to win the next game.

"We dropped two positions," Coach said. "And the reason for that is simple. We didn't play well in our last game. We may have won, but we didn't win convincingly."

Kevin poked me in the side and when I turned he mouthed *I told you.*

"We didn't win our game by enough points or with enough intensity. The people who made up the rankings decided we lacked something very important. We lacked the thing that separates the winners from the almost winners. We lacked killer instinct. We had that team down and beaten, and do you know what we did?" he asked.

I knew he wasn't looking for an answer.

"We let them up off the ground. We let them score a touchdown on us and we didn't score in the last quarter. We didn't finish them off. Do you know what that is out there?" he said, pointing to the field. "That," he said, "is a *war* zone. When we go out there, we aren't just playing a game. We are going into battle, we are going to war. And in a war there is no place for prisoners."

Of course I knew there were prisoners of war. But I also knew I'd have to be crazy to say anything.

"We all know we have a game on Thursday," he continued. "It's not enough to simply beat the other team. It's not enough for us to win. We have to *blow* them off the field, we have to *kill* them."

Somehow, after yesterday, the words *kill* and *blow them off the field* sounded a bit strange.

His voice cracked over the last words. When he got worked up, his voice got higher and higher until he sounded like he had been sucking helium. He sounded a bit like Minnie Mouse but nobody dared to smile. A voice shared with Minnie Mouse did not make for a good inspirational football speech.

I knew we'd win our game on Thursday. We were a much better team. But of course Coach Pruit was right. It wasn't enough for us just to win. We were expected to win. We had to win by a lot. And just like it wasn't enough for us just to win, it wasn't enough for us to be listed at number three in the rankings. Our school had a tradition of being the best at football. For other schools it was basketball, or baseball, or their science programs, or having the top students, or for their musical or drama programs. For us it was football. This might be the only school where being ranked second and losing in the finals would be considered a complete failure. We knew that. All the students and parents knew that. Mr. Pruit knew that too. And especially because this was his first year as head coach, he couldn't afford *not* to win it all.

"Okay, one lap of the track and then everybody change and get ready for class," Mr. Pruit said. "I'll see you men right here after school. Expect that practice will not be a picnic."

Slowly people got to their feet and started moving. Kevin moved to the front of the pack and I stayed at his side.

"Come on, pick it up!" Kevin yelled over his shoulder. "Move it, move it, move it!"

The whole line behind us jumped forward, picking up the pace. As we rounded the first corner, I looked back at the line of players snaking along behind us. Forty-two players, all in full pads and equipment, jogging along in a line. It felt like we were leading an army. And, I guess, in a way we were.

We finished the lap. The last stragglers, mostly the linemen, were still half a lap back. Kevin started walking back, yelling at them to hustle or they'd get another lap. I kept walking. Being first into the dressing room meant getting a shower right away and not having to wait in line. I unbuckled my helmet and pulled it off. I could feel the rush of cool air.

We came in through the back doors and our cleats clicked against the floor. It sounded ominous and powerful, and with each extra player coming in the sound got louder. Students in the hall moved out of our way. I didn't blame them. We *were* like an army and we were big guys—even bigger in our pads, helmets, and cleats.

I could tell we had finished up later than usual this morning because of the number of people in the hall.

I hoped there was time for a shower. I hated going to class all sweaty and smelly. I led the procession around the corner and it suddenly struck me. This was the corridor where the bomb disposal robot had been rolling along, where the locker had been searched. I wondered which locker belonged to the guy who'd been arrested.

Almost instantly, I had my answer. Four little orange pylons on the floor stood around a locker with the door gone, replaced by yellow police tape! All that remained of the door were twisted hinges. I pictured that police robot extending its big claw arm and just ripping the door off.

I slowed down and was bumped by the guy behind me. He was looking at the locker as well, instead of where he was walking. I stepped aside. I wanted to look longer. The line of players kept moving and I looked at the locker through them as they passed.

The locker was completely empty. Whatever had been in there was gone. There was a dusting of thin white powder on the bottom of the locker. For a split second I had the bizarre thought it was explosives or some sort of chemical—anthrax or the plague—but that was just crazy. More likely, it was something the police sprayed on to detect explosives, or to take fingerprints or—

"Excuse me."

"What?"

"Excuse me," a girl said. She was brown and little. She must have been in grade nine. "Could I get to my locker...please?"

"Oh...sure," I muttered.

I stepped out of the way and bumped into another girl.

"I'm sorry," she muttered, even though I was the one who had bumped into her.

"No, I'm sorry, it was my fault," I apologized as I shifted again.

She was even smaller than the first, and she wore a pink scarf and that funny sort of dress they wear sometimes. I suddenly felt very big and clumsy and out of place in all my football equipment.

"Pretty weird, huh?" I said, trying to be friendly.

She looked slightly up at me, hardly making eye contact, nodded her head a bit, and then looked away. It was almost like she was afraid of me.

"It's hard to believe that could happen here," I said, gesturing to the locker and police tape.

"*Impossible* to believe," a voice said from behind. I turned around. It was Zana—a girl I knew from my geography class. She had volunteered to be my partner last year for a project when I didn't know anybody else in the class. She was smart and friendly and had a great sense of humor. Right now, she didn't look that friendly.

"Hi. How are you doing?" I asked.

"Not so great. No way would Azeem be involved in anything like that," she said.

I shrugged. "I don't really know him."

"Well, I do. It's just not possible."

"Police must have had some reason."

"We'll see about that. We'll just have to wait until the truth comes out," she said.

The last few players were still moving down the hall. Kevin was at the end, talking to a couple of the linemen who were moving along slowly.

"Come on, Jay. Get shaking or you'll be late for class," Kevin said as he walked by.

"Yeah, sure." I started to walk away.

"Ask Mustafa about Azeem," Zana said.

I stopped and turned. "Mustafa?"

"Mustafa," she said, pointing to one of the linemen who had just passed by.

"Oh," I said nodding my head. *Moose.*

"His name is Mustafa."

Moose was one of two brown guys on the team. He was in grade twelve and I only knew him from the team. He was big, and not very fast, and his feet sort of pointed east and west when he was running north or south. He seemed like a pretty cool guy, though. He usually had an iPod in his pocket and at least one of the earphones in. He was always downloading new hip-hop songs that he wanted people to hear.

"Mustafa knows him," Zana said. "You ask him if Azeem could be a terrorist."

"Sure...thanks...I'll do that."

I trotted away. Time was tight. By the time I got to the locker room, there was already a line waiting for the showers. There probably wouldn't be enough time for me to have one. I'd just splash on a whole lot of body wash and hope one smell overpowered the other.

The locker room was loud and hot and smelly. If it all weren't so familiar, it would have been disgusting. I could hear the showers going and some of the guys were already finished, walking back wearing only towels. I sat down on the bench and started to peel off my uniform and equipment. Everything was sticky and wet with sweat. If it smelled now, it would be a lot worse after spending the day in my gym bag in the locker.

Moose was sitting on a bench across from me.

"Moose!" I called out.

His iPod was on, both ears plugged in. He didn't hear me.

"Moose!" I yelled, and waved.

He looked up and pulled out one of the plugs. "Yeah."

"That guy, Azeem. The one arrested. Do you know him?"

"Sure."

"And what do you think?"

"About what?" he asked.

"Do you think he could be guilty?"

He shrugged. "How would I know?"

"I just thought—"

"Because he's Muslim and I'm Muslim, I'd know?"

"No," I said, shaking my head, although that was at least part of it. "That girl I was talking to."

He looked confused.

"The one I was talking to in the hall just now."

"Aaahhh...yes...that's Zana...very pretty."

"Yeah, I guess. She said you knew him."

"I do. I just don't know him that well. I'm here at football practices and he's part of the prayer group."

"What prayer group?"

"Some Muslim kids, they meet in one of the shop classes and they study the Koran and say prayers. Lots of kids are part of that group. I go there myself sometimes."

That surprised me, although I didn't know why it should.

"Muslims are supposed to gather and say prayers five times a day," Moose explained. "One of those times is right around noon."

"And you go there to pray." I wasn't sure if that was a question or a statement.

"Sure. Sometimes. Most of the time I just go to McDonald's."

"You say prayers at McDonald's?"

Moose laughed. "The only thing I pray for there is that the lineup won't be too long at lunchtime."

This time I laughed too. I didn't really know Moose—Mustafa—as anything more than a lineman. Heck, other than knowing that he liked hip-hop I didn't know anything about him. I hadn't even known his real name until five minutes ago. What he did when he wasn't downloading music or playing football was a mystery to me. He could be going to study the Koran, working in the library, or helping the homeless. Or making bombs.

Moose plugged in the second earphone and continued to change out of his football stuff.

— ✳ —

I'd hoped there'd be more in the announcements. But all there was after the national anthem was the usual assortment of things about school clubs, drama night, the football game on Thursday, and somebody who had left on the headlights of their blue Ford Focus. Nothing about what had gone on yesterday. Not a thing. Yesterday was nothing more than a mass hallucination. The only evidence here at the school to the contrary was the locker and an empty seat in some grade-twelve class somewhere in the school.

I wondered where that Azeem guy was right now. Was he in court? In jail? How would he ever survive in jail? Not that I'd ever been, but I'd watched enough episodes of *Law & Order* and *Oz* to know it wasn't the best place in the world to be if you were weak and unable to defend yourself.

Suddenly the fire alarm started to ring. Some people groaned. Some seemed happy; it was an excuse to get out of class, see some friends, maybe wander over to the creek and have a smoke. We started to pack our bags. We weren't supposed to. We were supposed to just leave, but we all knew that it was just another false alarm, and we didn't want to have to come back to get our things. Somebody pulled the alarm at least once every couple of weeks.

"Okay, everybody. Please file out through the appropriate door," Mrs. Henderson said. She didn't sound any more worried or excited than any of the rest of us. Maybe she was looking forward to standing outside and talking to the other teachers.

"Please exit through stairway B," she said.

Somebody opened the door and the ringing got louder. There was a bell just outside our homeroom.

"Smoke!" somebody yelled out.

Instantly the other sounds stopped and all eyes turned to the door. There was a thin layer of smoke wafting through the air!

"Everyone out, immediately!" Mrs. Henderson yelled. Suddenly she wasn't so calm.

A few people hesitated, still packing their bags, but most people rushed for the door, creating a momentary traffic jam. I popped through and into the hall. There was smoke coming up the stairwell and filling the hall. It was thick and black.

This was for real.

Teachers lined the hall, hurrying people along. One girl tried to get into her locker but was hustled away. She started arguing about her new jacket being in there. Apparently, her jacket was more important than her life. Must be some jacket—or maybe not much of a life.

I followed the flow, along the hall, into the far stairwell and down to the first floor. I'd been in at least a dozen fire drills, but this was different. Everyone was moving faster; nobody was talking or joking around much. In fact, some of the kids and teachers seemed genuinely worried.

We exited the school and spilled out into the side parking lot. The crowd started to fan out and slow down, but the teachers kept everyone moving away from the school and onto the football field. There was already a crowd gathering in the center of the field as streams of students flowed from different doors.

I turned around and looked back at the school. I didn't see anything. Certainly no fire. I looked around for Kevin. For a split second I had the bizarre idea that he was up on the roof, watching. That was crazy. Not even Kevin would do that.

At that instant the fire truck appeared. It had its

lights on but it didn't seem to be moving very quickly. They probably thought it was just another false alarm. Firemen must hate false alarms. They must hate high schools. This time, though, it was for real. Somebody had set a fire—or set off a bomb.

Now, that was even crazier thinking than wondering if Kevin was on the roof, watching. No way had there been a bomb. I would have heard it...wouldn't I? But what if Azeem hadn't kept the bomb in his locker but in somebody else's locker—or somewhere else around the school? And whoever was in on it with him decided that the best way to free Azeem was to set off the bomb while he was in custody. Or maybe it went off by accident, or someone set it off because he was angry that his friend had been arrested or— I stopped myself. What was I thinking? Probably somebody had dropped a cigarette butt into a garbage can.

The fire truck came to a stop with the piercing, squealing sound of its brakes. Three police cars pulled up behind. Casually the firemen got off the truck. Two of them, wearing thick coats, big black boots, and helmets, walked toward the side exit. One of them pulled open a door.

Black smoke came billowing out and into the sky.

Two firefighters pulled on masks. On their backs were air tanks. They ducked down low and stepped through the door and into the building.

"Wow," I muttered to myself. Firemen amazed me. How brave would you have to be to walk into a burning building?

Another fireman used an axe to wedge open the door. It took a while before the first two firefighters reappeared. One of them held a small container. Smoke was billowing out of it. Instantly I knew what it was.

A smoke bomb.

Somebody had set off a smoke bomb in the stairwell.

The fireman dropped it to the ground and another fireman aimed the nozzle of a fire extinguisher at it. A line of white foam shot out, beating down the smoke, covering it, smothering it, entombing the fire in a pile of white foam. A final puff of smoke drifted up into the sky and the smoke bomb was no more.

"Somebody set off a smoke bomb," I said, more to myself than the people around me.

"At least it got us out of French," somebody beside me said.

Getting out of French did sound pretty good. It just better not mean that there was no football practice tonight. If it did get canceled, I wasn't going to drive home with Kevin. It would be a lot safer to walk home.

CHAPTER SIX

HAROON

"DID WE CREATE GOD, or did God create us?"

Ms. Singh is standing in front of our comparative religions class, her face joyful at presenting us with an unanswerable question. Our desks are in a large circle, so that she can see all of us and we can all see each other.

"How many of you believe that God created us?" she asks the class.

Many kids raise their hands. Ms. Singh has them all go to one end of the room, calling them Group A.

"How many of you think that *we* created God?"

I put my hand up, then take it down, then put it up again, then take it down. Ms. Singh sees me.

"How many of you are not sure?"

I can certainly raise my hand to that. My family is religious, but we also believe in science. There are a few other hands in the air.

"Group A, you will come up together with a list of compelling reasons why Group B is right. Group B, you will do the same to prove Group A's position. Group C, the undecideds, you will come up with a list of what makes a religion. You have fifteen minutes in your groups, then we will come back together and share."

Ms. Singh does that a lot, gets us to argue someone else's point of view. My group starts off strong, with things like shared philosophy, belief in the supernatural, rituals, organization of behavior. Then someone mentions Jim Jones and Hare Krishna, and wonders what the difference is between a religion and a cult. We try then to divide the list between good religion and bad religion. By the time our fifteen minutes are up, we are even more confused than when we started, but we have lots to think about.

Ms. Singh asks me to stay behind for a moment when the class ends. I've been dreading this, but I knew it was coming. With Azeem arrested, there is an opening on the team.

"José dropped out," she says. "His mother called me. She's upset that her son was 'cavorting with a terrorist.' That's how she put it. 'Cavorting with a terrorist.' It's not a phrase you hear every day."

"Have you heard what kids are saying?" I ask her. "About me?"

She nods. "Is it true?"

"What? No!"

"Well, then?"

I hesitate.

"I hope you won't take this long to answer when you're on television."

"I'll do it," I say.

She smiles. "It will be fine," she says. "It will be more than fine. We're going to win this year!"

The bell rings, and I race off to my next class, eager to disappear into the impersonal, nonreligious confusion of algebra.

Zana and I are both in this class. In one way, I'm glad, because she goes over the work with me at home. It's the only way I've managed to maintain a B. On the other hand, having her nearly perfect scores pointed out after every test makes it painfully obvious who is the smarter of the two of us. I'm smarter than Zana in some things, but not in algebra, or anything that involves that type of puzzle-solving thinking. There are too many threads to keep track of. Zana is like some mad weaver, keeping all the threads in place, pulling them out as she needs them. I suppose memory is my biggest strength. That's probably why I was the one chosen for the *Reach for the Top* team.

In class, I sit two rows across and three seats down from her. I can watch the back of her head during the lesson. I can almost see all that data flowing into her brain and linking up with all the other data that's there.

Today is mostly review for an upcoming test. Our teacher this year is big on review. "It only gets harder," she says. "If you miss a step, you'll get lost in the dance." Thanks to Zana's coaching, I'm able to follow today's work. It's even a relief to write figures in my notebook, tidy and clear, to know that there *is* a right answer, and that I might even be able to find it.

The class is concentrating deeply, our heads bent over our books, occasionally glancing up at the front as our teacher leads us, almost mantra-like, through the jumble to a clear, logical pattern. The answer is right there, just a few steps away. I know what the steps are and I know how to do them. I am inches, seconds away from solving the puzzle.

And then the fire alarm goes off.

It is so loud and sudden, and we have been so quiet and focused, a few of the kids actually let out little screams. I don't scream but I do jump, my pen making a dark, ugly mark through the lovely row of figures. I look down at my notebook in despair. The equation now makes no sense, the threads all dropped and burned.

"Class, stand."

We stand by our desks and, row by row, file out into the hall.

"This is not a time for talking," a teacher says, as he herds us down the nearest staircase. "Stay with your class out in the schoolyard."

Of course, none of us does. The language teachers try to continue oral drills outside. We hear chants of

"A falta de pan buenas son las tortas" coming from the Spanish class, and equally useful phrases from the French class. Most of the teachers don't bother trying. We're all told at the beginning of the year that students who don't return to class after fire drill are marked absent. It saves the teachers trying to chase after escapees.

Julian finds me. He's in his smock from art class. It's covered with paint. "Looks like the real thing," he says, as a fire truck comes up the street and stops in front of the school. Students cheer. Are they cheering because the fire truck is here or because the school is burning down?

Police cars follow the fire truck.

"Look!" someone yells, pointing up at the school. Smoke is pouring out of some of the windows.

"This could take a while," I say to Julian. We make ourselves comfortable on a low wall by the teachers' parking lot. Julian is the type of friend who likes companionable silence as much as good conversation. We've known each other for years. We go on long hikes along the river, sometimes not talking for ages, then one of us will pull a thought from the air, maybe from a conversation we'd had weeks ago, and we slide right into it as if there had never been a pause.

We watch the police and firefighters run around. After a bit, I get tired of watching them and start watching the students.

"It's the herd mentality," I say.

"Deer to deer? Goat to goat?"

"Even the teacher animals hang together."

It's true. Some teachers are still with their classes, but most are standing around in a lump. Some look like they wish they could smoke, but smoking areas are strictly enforced at our school, and the principal doesn't like teachers to smoke at all in front of students.

It isn't universal, but it's clear enough to make a statement. The jocks have drifted to be with other jocks. The rockers are with the other leather and metal kids. The car guys and their girlfriends are draped around each other over by the recycling bins. The Caribbean kids are together, the science fiction kids are together, and the loners are scattered around, trying to look like they don't mind being alone.

"Remember when we were little kids?" Julian asks. "A kid was a kid was a kid."

"When did we start to notice differences?" I wonder.

"That's the *real* loss of innocence, man."

Another cheer goes up. We see a couple of fire-fighters come out of the building, one holding a smoke bomb.

Two cops are suddenly beside me. Detective Moffett and the driver who had talked to me yesterday. The driver speaks in a loud, clear voice.

"If you knew about this, Haroon, and didn't tell us, we will hold you criminally responsible."

They walk away without waiting for my denial. It's just as well, because words are failing me once again. I look at all the faces staring at me, their expressions full of question. I do not know what to say to them. Julian pulls me away, but I can still feel their eyes on me.

"They're just playing with you," Julian says. "Don't let them get to you."

I'm about to say something tough and blustery, which neither of us will believe, but will help me pretend to feel better, when Zana appears and says, "Can't you *ever* speak up for yourself?"

We are allowed back into the school. I feel small and powerless and an outsider among my own classmates.

CHAPTER SEVEN

JAY

PRACTICE HAPPENED. Halfway through, I was starting to wish it hadn't. Coach wasn't in a good mood.

I was getting used to the pattern. Every practice that was closer to the actual game day made him tenser, more difficult. Then, the day after the game, he was more relaxed, almost nice. Of course, we'd won every game. I didn't want to find out what he'd be like the day after a loss. Maybe that would be the day *I'd* set off a smoke bomb in the locker room so we wouldn't have to find out.

That's all it had been—a smoke bomb. I'd found out that I wasn't the only person who had thought about it being a bomb. Lots of students had thought that. So had some of the teachers. Maybe after what had happened it wasn't such a stupid idea after all.

Instead, it had been some stupid kid who had set it off in the stairwell. Right in the stairwell, right in front of one of the school surveillance cameras mounted up on the wall. It was all there for the office to see. Of course, I hadn't seen the video, but one of

84

the teachers who had seen it told another teacher who told us. Yesterday we were like a scene from *Law & Order* and had been on the real news. Today we were like a bad reality show. America's Stupidest Videos.

The kid must have known there was a camera. I'd heard that he had pulled his shirt up to cover his face. He wasn't very big—they said he looked like a grade niner. Odds were that he was just doing it to get out of class or some test he didn't want to take. If they caught him, he'd get his wish. There'd be no more classes and no more tests. He'd be suspended for the rest of the semester.

Funny. All of this happened today, just a few hours ago. Everybody knew all about it. They knew about the video. They knew how tall he was and what he was wearing. But what about yesterday? All day I had waited for somebody—the principal, a teacher, anybody—to make some kind of announcement. Instead, there was nothing official. And without anything official, everybody just talked.

Rumor instead of fact.

Some of the talk had been about the prayer room. I found out it was one of the shop classes that wasn't used that much. It was a room right off the corridor, where a bunch of brown kids had their lockers. Moose had told me that Muslims were supposed to pray five times a day. That seemed a little excessive to me. You'd figure that God might have better things to do then be bothered that many times every day. They said prayers in the shop room and talked about their Bible, the Koran, which was like their Bible. The whole thing sounded like going to church every day. One day, Sunday, was more than enough for anybody as far as I was concerned. Thank goodness my parents didn't even make me go that often. Every second or third week was enough for them. And they only made me go at Christmas and Easter and a few extra times thrown in for good measure.

"You coming, or what?" Kevin asked as he stood holding the door to the change room open.

"Just gotta go to my locker for a second."

"Come on, let's get moving. Steve's probably already out by the car."

I threw my things into a gym bag and hurried off for my locker. We headed down the hall. It was quiet. I liked that. We passed by the brown corridor lockers.

"Quite the smell," I said.

"Yeah, this hall always stinks. I think it's something those people eat, like curry or something...it *oozes* out of their pores."

"I meant the smoke," I said.

"Oh...yeah, the smoke. That kid was an idiot."

"Yeah, that was pretty stupid, setting off a smoke bomb in a school."

"No," Kevin said, "I didn't mean setting off the

86

smoke bomb. I meant setting it off right in front of a security camera. If he'd been smart, he would have set it off on the second floor and dropped it down the stairwell. There's no camera on the second floor stairwell."

"Sounds like you've been thinking about this."

He shook his head. "I just know where the cameras are."

We stopped in front of my locker. I undid the lock and as I opened it up some books fell from the top shelf. I tried, and failed, to catch them before they dropped to the floor.

"Ever wonder why you're playing linebacker instead of receiver?" Kevin asked.

"I can catch," I said as I picked up the books and put them back into the locker. "I just think it's better to give than receive. Receivers get hit and linemen do the hitting."

"Much better to hit than get hit."

"No argument there. I'd love to put a couple of licks on somebody sometime, but the QB doesn't get that chance very often."

I grabbed a couple of t-shirts from the bottom of the locker, some sweat socks, and a pair of sneakers.

"Wow," Kevin said, "it's a good thing the police dogs didn't check out this locker. With their sensitive snouts they might have passed out."

"Like it's worse than your locker."

"My locker smells like *my* sweat. Nobody minds

the smell of their own sweat...sort of like how you never think your own farts smell bad."

"Sometimes you amaze me," I said.

Kevin grinned. "Sometimes I even amaze myself."

I slammed the locker closed. The halls were completely empty now and the caretakers had even turned off the lights in some of the corridors. Schools —empty schools—sort of spooked me. We opened the door to the stairwell—the stairwell where the smoke bomb had been set off. The smell of smoke was much, much stronger.

"Did you know that Moose's real name is Mustafa?" I asked.

"Yeah. You didn't?"

"No."

"Did you think his parents named him Moose?"

"Of course not. I just figured it was a nickname because he's so big, like a moose."

"He's not that big," Kevin said. "Moose and I go way back. We were in the same grade one class. Moose is a good guy."

"Yeah, he is. Did you know he goes to that shop class sometimes to say prayers?"

"I didn't know that. I guess there's nothing wrong with that."

"I didn't say there was," I said. "It just seems strange."

"Do you ever say prayers?" Kevin asked.

"Of course. At meals...church...the usual." I also said prayers every night, but I wasn't going to admit that to him.

"Wave to the camera," Kevin said as we hit the first floor.

I didn't wave, but I did look up at it. I was going to start noticing all those cameras. Not that I was going to do anything I needed to hide from. I read somewhere that if you worked or lived in the city, just walking around or driving and shopping, that you could be on dozens and dozens of different cameras every day. I guess there were good reasons to have those cameras everywhere. I'd heard that ever since 9/11, there were a lot more of them. That made perfect sense to me. What was wrong with being on video if you weren't doing anything wrong?

Kevin's car was one of the last left in the parking lot. Steve was sitting on the hood. Sort of a big, black hood ornament.

"I got shotgun," Steve said.

He said that every time. I never argued. As far as I was concerned, he deserved to be up front. He was assistant captain, a senior, and a longtime friend of Kevin's. I was still the new guy.

"I have to make a stop," Kevin said as we started away.

"Where?"

"I have to pick up something at the mall. Won't take long."

The mall was just up ahead and on the way home. I didn't have any place I was going to anyways. Kevin curved off the road and into the mall parking lot.

"This is the worst parking lot in the world," he said.

"It's always pretty crowded," I agreed.

"Not just crowded. Crowded with the world's worst drivers. Look at this idiot."

He slowed down and then brought the car to a stop behind another vehicle. It was sitting right in front of Wal-Mart, by the entrance, two feet away from the curb, blocking the lane so you had to swing into the line of oncoming traffic to get by.

"What the hell does she think she's doing, parking her car right there, blocking off traffic?" Kevin fumed.

We could see through the back window of the car that there were two women—one driving, the other in the passenger seat. They were both wearing big swirling scarves.

"Stupid idiot…can't drive because she can't see past that thing twisted around her head. Must be on so tight it's blocking the flow of blood to her brain."

He waited as cars coming in the other direction passed through the one open lane.

The last car passed and he swung out into the open lane before anybody else could come from the other direction. To my surprise, he slammed on the brakes, bringing the car to a stop right beside the offending vehicle. He leaned over so he could look past Steve and through the open windows of both vehicles.

"Hey!" Kevin screamed, and the driver turned. She was wearing a thick scarf that not only covered her head but most of her face as well.

"What are you waiting for?" he demanded. "Can't you read the sign? It says no parking! You should be riding a camel instead of driving that piece of crap. Get it moving—unless you're planning a suicide bombing!"

Through the narrow slit in her headgear, I saw her eyes widen in shock, and then fear. She rapidly started to roll up her window.

Kevin rocketed the car forward, and with a squeal of rubber we left them behind. He started laughing wildly. I found myself laughing too, even as I slouched down in my seat. He hung a quick turn down an aisle, driving way too fast for a parking lot. He saw an empty spot and spun the car in, almost hitting a grocery cart that was off to the side in the space.

"Perfect parking job," he said as the car came to a stop. All of the anger he'd just been spewing was completely gone. "Are you impressed?"

"You really went off on her," Steve said.

"She was blocking traffic."

"Which was way different than what you did when you stopped beside her, right?" Steve asked.

"You wanna be a back-seat driver, I might have to start putting you into the back seat. I was performing a service. Probably couldn't read the sign because she doesn't speak any English."

We climbed out of the car. I looked over to where the car had been. It was gone now, but there was another car pulled off to the side just up from where that car had been sitting.

"Lots of people park there and block the way," Steve said.

I noticed them too when I'd been here at the mall with my parents.

"Just because lots of people do it doesn't make it right. Besides, people shouldn't be able to drive wearing those stupid things on their heads. How can they see?"

That was the same argument I'd heard my father use more than once.

"I don't get the suicide bomber part. What did that mean?" Steve questioned.

"*That* was stupid," Kevin agreed. "No way in the world one of those people would ever blow up a Wal-Mart. They practically *live* at Wal-Mart."

He had a point. I didn't go to Wal-Mart very

often, but when I did, it seemed like everybody in the place was from someplace other than here.

"Maybe Wal-Mart has a special section for them to get their head wear...probably beside the bedding section. Don't some of those things look like bedding?"

I smiled. Some of them did.

"And another section, right beside the linens, would be where those guys can get towels for their heads."

"Those aren't Arabs. Those are Sikhs, aren't they?" I asked.

"Sikhs, Arabs, same difference."

I shook my head. "Arabs are Muslims and Sikhs aren't. They're from India...which makes them sort of Hindi, I think."

"Since when are you an expert on religions?" Kevin demanded. He didn't sound happy.

I should have kept my mouth closed to begin with. "I'm no expert." This was getting uncomfortable. "What are you picking up?"

"I hope it's food," Steve said. "I'm hungry."

"It is food. *Dog* food."

"I'm not *that* hungry," Steve joked.

There was an outside door to Pet Valu and we walked in. We followed Kevin down the aisle. He picked up a gigantic bag of food and tossed it onto his shoulder. He brought it up to the front counter and paid for it with his debit card.

"I got it," Steve said as he picked up the bag and put it on his shoulder. "Wow, this is heavy. This is one big bag."

"I got one big dog."

"How much *does* Bruno weigh?" I asked.

"He comes in at around one hundred and thirty pounds."

"If I didn't know he was gentle he'd be scary," I said.

I had been a bit spooked the first time that dog came bouncing toward me. He was gigantic.

"He wouldn't harm a fly, but people don't know that." Kevin chuckled. "I had him out for a run yesterday, had him off his leash at the park. There were some Chinese people walking through, and Bruno went running up to say hello. They started screaming and yelling. It was hilarious!"

"I don't get it. Why are those people always afraid of dogs?" Steve asked.

"Doesn't make sense to me," Kevin agreed. "It's not like they never saw a dog before. Heck, it's not like they've never *eaten* a dog before."

"Maybe they're afraid that dogs are looking to bite *them* before they can bite the dogs." Steve started laughing and then began talking in a mock-Chinese accent. "You gimme order of pork fried rice, side order of *poodle*."

Both Kevin and I laughed. Steve was one of the funniest people I knew.

"I thought they just ate cat," I added.

"*All* house pets," Kevin said. "My cousin told me a story about this Asian kid in his class when he was in grade two. Over Christmas, different kids took home the class pets. They had some mice and a couple of gerbils and a rabbit. Anyways, this little Asian kid takes home the rabbit. Christmas holidays end and the kid brings back a thank-you note from his parents thanking the teacher for their Christmas meal!"

"That's gross!" Steve yelled. "Do you think that really happened?"

"My cousin swears!" Kevin said.

"And how about that Chinese restaurant downtown that was busted? The health inspector found dead cats and dogs hanging in the freezer," Steve said.

"So you could have a spot of tea and a spot of *Spot*," Kevin laughed.

Kevin popped the trunk and Steve tossed the bag of dog food in. We climbed into the car.

"Sounds like an urban myth to me," Steve said. "You know, everybody knows somebody who knows somebody who saw it on the news."

Kevin started to back up and then had to slam on the brakes as a car whizzed by. "I got an urban myth for you," Kevin said. "Did you hear about the Chinese driver who actually *could* drive?"

"That *is* a myth," Steve agreed, "although I don't know anybody who knows anybody who's ever seen that."

"DWA," I said.

"What?" Kevin asked.

"DWA. Driving While Asian." That was what my father called it. Chinese drivers drove him crazy. There were no Chinese drivers back home.

They both started laughing.

"Do you know how every racist joke starts?" Kevin asked.

I shook my head.

He turned his head slightly and looked over my shoulder and then the other.

I started laughing.

"I don't get it," Steve said.

"I'm checking to see who's behind me before I start telling the joke...get it?"

"Okay, now I get it. Too bad it wasn't funny."

"And you can do better?"

"Sure. How do you know when your house has been robbed by Asian burglars?" Steve asked.

"I give up," Kevin said. "How?"

"The cat is missing, your kid's math homework has been done, the computer has been de-bugged, and they're still trying to back out of the driveway."

"You really *are* a racist," Kevin said and started laughing.

"Me? How can I be a racist? I'm black."

"Last time I checked your mother was white."

"She's just really, *really* light skinned."

"She has blonde hair," Kevin said.

"Dye job."

"And blue eyes and she's Swedish, isn't she?"

"You saying there's nobody black in Sweden?"

"I'm not even sure there's anybody in Sweden who has *black* hair," Kevin said.

"All I can think of are beautiful, tall, blonde babes playing volleyball," I said.

"That is a very fine image," Kevin agreed. "Bouncing up and down—"

"You white guys just don't get it," Steve said.

"Us white guys?" Kevin asked.

"Yeah, you know who you are. You haven't lived the pain of slavery, being denied your rights, the prejudice I experience because of the color of my skin. Shouldn't a man be judged by his character rather than the color of his skin?"

Steve was joking around...wasn't he? I couldn't tell by his tone or his expression, but he couldn't be serious—could he?

"You're right about judging people by their character," Kevin agreed. "And you are one big *character*. Steve, you crack me up."

"The only crack I know is the sound of the white man's whip against my skin."

"Steve, you are such a—"

"And that's another thing. Stop calling me Steve. That's my slave name."

Steve suddenly broke into a big grin and started laughing.

"I can think of a few other things I could call you, but then I'd be a racist. Do you want to shut up now or do I have to put you in the trunk with the dog food?"

"I'll stay quiet, master, sir. Sure wouldn't want no uppity blacks talking back to the white folks. Not enough you want us in the back of the bus, you want us in the trunk of the bus!"

I'd heard Steve do this sort of routine a dozen times.

"Do people ever really give you a hard time about being black?" I asked.

"Some people are jerks. Nobody who matters does, and that's all that matters."

"But what about the racial jokes…do they bother you?"

"Depends. I like racial jokes…unless they're black jokes. Those jokes aren't funny." He paused. "Unless somebody black says them."

His expression and voice were completely serious, almost ominous. I suddenly regretted getting this started.

"Everybody else better watch their mouths,"

Steve said, "and that includes you two honky crackers!" he said, pointing a finger first at Kevin and then at me. "If you know what's good for you, you'll just watch your mouths. I'm carrying and I could cut you!"

He suddenly reached into this pocket and pulled out a set of nail clippers.

"Damn! I thought all black people carried a knife!" Steve said. He held the little clippers up in the air. "This would have been way more dramatic if it had been a knife, but still, one more word from either of you and I'm gonna give you a manicure! I could still cut you bad! I could do some serious damage to your cuticles."

We all started laughing.

"And, Kevin, could you stop on the way home so I could get some KFC? You know how us black folks just *loves* our chicken! If you could get me some of that KFC, that would make me so happy I just might break into a song and start shuffling and dancing."

CHAPTER EIGHT

JAY

"HAVE YOU SEEN THIS?" Kevin demanded as he practically shoved a newspaper into my face.

"What, did somebody get traded?" Steve asked as he reached for the paper.

"No! Not the sports section. This!"

I took the paper from his hand. It was today's paper and he had it folded open to one of the four or five pages that were devoted to the arrest of the terrorists. I'd read some of the stories. I'd read everything yesterday and watched the entire news on TV, but it seemed like there were no new arrests or anything different to report. The papers and newscasters were just spinning the same story, like they had to report it but had nothing new to report. Like writing an essay when you don't really know what you're talking about.

"Look, right here!" Kevin said, stabbing the paper with his finger.

There was a little sidebar article underneath the picture of three people—teenagers…brown teenagers. The heading said Understands Why They Did It.

I scanned down the column of print. It was an interview with some Muslim teenagers. They were saying that they were surprised by the arrests, and thought that those people who were arrested were innocent.

"Let me read it to you," Kevin said, practically ripping the paper from my hands. "It's right here. Husain Multar, seventeen, says, 'I know one of them, and I know that he is a good Muslim and therefore not guilty of the charges. His arrest is the result of persecution of Muslims by the police and government, and he would have been subject to prejudice and inhumane treatment that all Muslims receive at *school* from whites.'"

"Haven't I been saying the same thing?" Steve said. "Those whites are all devils."

"Shut up, Steve. As far as he's concerned, you're white too."

Steve held his hand up, turned it over slowly, staring at it. "I beg to differ. I'm pretty sure I'm black—half Swedish black."

"You're no different than me or Jay or an albino," Kevin said. He ran his finger down the page, trying to find his place. "Here it is. *All* non-Muslims are racist, and Muslims are the target of discrimination based on their faith. White students at my school treat the Muslims badly and exclude them from school life. I am not liked or accepted because of my religion."

"Maybe he isn't liked because he's a jerk," Steve said.

"You got that right." Kevin scowled. "Now get this. 'I do not believe in bombs. But I understand why it might be necessary to build a bomb or have weapons to defend the faith against the aggression of infidels.'" Kevin paused. "And, here's the kicker. It says right here that this kid goes to Central Secondary School."

"He goes to our school?" Steve said.

Kevin nodded and his scowl grew. "Bad enough we have a terrorist going to the school without some yahoo defending him and telling the world that it's all *our* fault."

"It's stupid," I agreed. "But there's not much you can do about it."

"Oh yeah? Come with me."

Kevin turned and started walking away. Steve fell in behind him. I didn't know what he was going to do, but I knew there would be some action and I wanted to see it in person instead of hear about it. I trotted down the hall and fell into step beside him.

"Where are we going?"

"I'm not going to let any sand monkey go around insulting our school," he added loudly.

I looked around to see if any sand monkeys had heard him.

Nothing. Nobody. No reaction.

"Keep in mind a fight could get you suspended," Steve said.

"I'm just going to use my words. Nothing wrong with talking," he said.

"All depends on what you're going to say," Steve said.

"Not much. I'm just going to tell him to keep his mouth shut."

"What are you going to do if he doesn't want to shut up?" Steve asked.

"He'll shut up."

We steamed through the hall.

I knew we were heading to one of two places— either the brown corridor or Brown Town. As we walked, we passed other guys from the football team. Kevin and Steve invited them to join in. Soon there were six, then seven, then ten guys walking together. I was safely sealed off in the center of the pack.

That's what it felt like—a pack.

With each new addition, it seemed like we were walking faster, that we had more power, more strength. Kids in the hall just flattened themselves against the lockers and got out of our way. It was a rush.

What would Husain say, how would he react when Kevin came up to him and wanted to talk? Would this end up in a brawl between us and a bunch of brown guys? No. When Kevin started talking, it was more likely the kid would wet his pants than fight.

Or he might pull out a weapon.

That last thought made me hesitate for a half step. They said on the news that they were still looking for more suspects, and this kid did get quoted as saying he understood why people needed to carry weapons. What if he had a knife or a gun?

Kevin came to a halt and the line behind stopped. We were standing in the brown corridor. There were kids at their lockers, or standing in little clusters and talking. At first, they didn't notice us. Then, little by little, the noise level died down and stopped completely. The brown kids all stood there staring at us— or trying hard not to stare.

"I'm looking for my good friend Husain Multar!" Kevin yelled out. "I'm hoping he could sign my newspaper." He held it up. "Sort of an autograph."

Nobody said anything.

"Has anybody seen him today?" Kevin demanded.

There was silence and Zana stepped forward.

"He's not here," she said. Her voice was calm and clear and she stared straight at Kevin. I had to hand it to her. If I hadn't been standing with the pack, there was no way I'd be standing up to it. If I were brown, I would have tried to make myself unseen and unheard.

"Do you know where he is?" Kevin snapped.

"He didn't come to school today," she said.

"Smart move after saying stupid things like this," Kevin said, holding up the newspaper. "If you're going to insult somebody, you should at least have the guts to say it to their face. Or at least show up to back up your words. Anybody here have anything they want to say to me?"

I thought for a split second that Zana might say something. I was glad when she didn't. There was complete silence. The few eyes that had been looking our way were all averted, suddenly finding the lockers or floor much more interesting. I couldn't blame them. I wouldn't have wanted to fight Kevin. Especially not when he was standing at the front of what looked like a mob.

"I want everybody to pass on to good old *Husain* that I'm going to be looking for him when he returns to school."

Kevin turned and walked back through the pack. We stepped aside as he passed and then joined in, letting him lead us away.

— ✳ —

"Excuse the interruption" came the voice over the PA. "Could the members of the football team please report to Gym Two for a short team meeting."

I knew that every eye was on me as I stood up. It felt good. Being a football player at this school was

105

something special. Occasionally we got called down to the gym for special meetings or sometimes we'd leave early for an away game. I didn't care what it was for; I was just grateful to be getting out of class.

The halls were empty except for other members of the team. Coach Pruit was probably going to give us another one of his speeches—he'd be all hyped up and try to get us hyped up as well. Not because he thought we were in danger of losing but because he wanted us to kill the other team. If only his voice didn't sound like he was sucking helium, those speeches might have worked better.

I filed into the gym. It was already half filled with more guys coming in from different doors. We all gave high fives, tapped hands, or just nodded our greetings. It was a pretty good bunch of guys.

"Can everybody please take a seat in the bleachers."

It was Principal Atkins. Standing beside him were both vice-principals, Mrs. Willis and Mr. Spence. Had something happened to Coach? I had been wondering if he was going to give himself a coronary over these games.

"We're going to keep this short," Mr. Atkins said. "I have had some disturbing reports about an altercation in the back hall this morning."

My heart rose up into my throat and then sank back down to the pit of my stomach.

"I have been told that members of the football

team gathered in the back hall and were intimidating other students."

There was a bit of grumbling from the bleachers. Besides the bunch of us who had been there, almost everybody else had heard about it.

"The reports are that a student—a Muslim student—was targeted by members of the football team."

"Nobody targeted anybody," Kevin said. "I was there."

"You were more than simply there," the principal said. "According to the reports you were the spokesperson for the group."

"I was talking, but it wasn't like the whole football team or anything," he said, gesturing to the team in the bleachers. "It was just me and a couple of the guys who wandered over to the back corridor. I wanted to talk to Husain."

"Is Husain a friend of yours?"

"Wouldn't know him if he bit me. I wanted to meet him to talk about the things he said in the paper. To tell him he was wrong. To find out why he thinks he doesn't belong. No prejudice here on the football team," Kevin said. "Look around."

There were lots of black faces to go along with the white ones, two brown kids—Moose and Ali—and one Chinese kid.

"Nobody threatened anybody," Kevin said.

"And you don't think that simply asking to speak

to him couldn't be taken as intimidation?" the principal asked.

"I can't tell you what anybody is thinking," Kevin said. "But nobody threatened anybody. I just wanted to talk."

"Talking is good. In fact, I wish there could be more dialogue about this whole thing. What I need is for members of this team to take a leadership role in helping to keep things calm and orderly and *normal* around the school." He paused. "So I'm going to ask that members of the team refrain from assembling in the hall by the shop classes. I would ask that the Muslim prayer room be respected."

Kevin put up his hand.

"How about Moose? Can he go to the prayer room?"

"Of course, Moose is Muslim."

"And a member of the football team," Kevin said. "Anybody can try out for the football team. There's no prejudice on who gets picked or how they're treated." Kevin turned to Moose. "Right, Mustafa?"

"No complaints from me. But I'm okay about not going to the prayer room if it would help."

"No, that won't be necessary," the principal said. "I'm just trying to keep the school running without incident. We're trying to avoid anything that might be misinterpreted."

"So do you want us to not talk to anybody who's brown?" Steve asked.

"Talking is fine, but please avoid topics that might be contentious or potentially explosive."

I didn't think that explosive was the best choice of words.

Kevin put up his hand.

"Yes, Kevin," he said. There was a tone in his voice, like he was just hoping that Kevin would shut up.

"So I guess it would be really bad for people to make statements like all Muslims are bad, right?"

"That goes without saying."

"How about a statement like all whites and non-Muslims are racists?" Kevin asked.

The principal suddenly realized where Kevin was going with this question.

"Or how about somebody saying it was okay to carry weapons to defend themselves—you know, because all whites are racist—or maybe to defend the Muslim faith. Wouldn't that be, you know, contentious or potentially explosive?"

There was a ripple of conversation as different people all at once realized what Kevin was saying. Clever.

"All those who say anything that even hints at intolerance or racism will be punished."

"So has Husain been punished?" Kevin asked.

"We are not here to discuss our reaction to the newspaper article," he said. "We are here to discuss any other reactions. If there are incidents, we will be taking clear and decisive actions, including suspensions, and if necessary, expulsion."

"For everybody?" Kevin asked.

"Everybody. Christian, Muslim, Jewish...even captains of the football team. Does that answer your question?"

"Completely," Kevin said. "And you can count on our help in following those rules." Kevin turned to face the team. "Right, everybody?"

Everybody shouted out in agreement.

This was good. Much better than what could have happened if Kevin had found Husain.

CHAPTER NINE

HAROON

IT'S JULIAN WHO COMES UP with the idea to go to Azeem's court appearance.

"We know him," he says. "We should be there to show some support. His family will be there, but they'll be all weeping and worried. He'll be glad to see a couple of normal people."

It sounds like the right thing to do, even though we'll have to cut classes to go. I tell my parents about it that evening. They're both home for dinner. Mom has barbecued some chicken. Zana sits across the table from me, as always, but doesn't look at me.

"I don't want you mixed up in this," my father says as he dishes out salad.

"I'm already mixed up in it. You should see the looks I get at school."

"This family is not ruled by looks, or by other people's opinions." My mother is agreeing with my father. They disagree on a million little things, but they always come together for the big ones. I'm a little worried that they see this as a big thing. *I* think it is, but I'd feel better if they thought it wasn't. Their judgment is pretty good, even though they don't know what it's like to be in high school these days.

"So what are we ruled by? The right to a fair trial?" I say. "The right to be presumed innocent until you're proven guilty?"

"Someone's been doing his homework," my father says.

"Azeem's right to a fair trial does not depend on you being in the courtroom," Mom says. "I don't want you anywhere near this. All around the world, people live in chaos. If our parents had stayed in Afghanistan, this family would be living in the middle of war and squalor and craziness and I don't know what. They didn't want that for themselves, and we don't want that for you. We're living well in a safe community. We believe in order and good manners."

"We're also Muslims," Zana says, the first words she's spoken since we sat down at dinner. "Or doesn't that count for anything?"

"Your mother just spent her whole day off preparing for Ramadan, so don't give us that attitude," Dad says.

"What preparing? Chopping vegetables? Shopping? Ramadan is a spiritual time, and we treat it like a social holiday," Zana says. "Why not just put up a Christmas tree and hang up a picture of Santa Claus? That's all Ramadan means to us."

"Is this the same daughter who refused to fast last year because it was—what did she say?—an 'archaic, patriarchal directive?'" Mom asks.

Zana has a great talent for ignoring anything that doesn't fit her current point of view. She waves aside Mom's comments. "They want us to assimilate. They want us to be more like them. That way, they can go after the people who are different."

"Who's 'they'?" Dad asks.

I keep out of it. I bend low over my plate, while the words fly around me. My mother makes amazing barbecue sauce, with curry and cilantro and oranges. She doesn't have time to cook very often, and I'm determined not to let one of Zana's arguments ruin my enjoyment of the meal.

As I eat, I'm able to block a lot of the argument out, but then Zana says, "One person being a coward makes it harder for everyone."

I hear that all right, and when I look up at her, there's no doubt she means that I am the coward.

My appetite is gone, and I leave the table.

Later, when they've all gone to their separate corners, I come out of my room and do the cleanup. (I'm not being nice. It's my turn.) Scrubbing, rinsing, putting food away. It's soothing. I wish all messes could be cleared up this easily.

When the work is done, I phone Julian.

"Let's go," I say. It's the right thing to do. I'll deal

with the consequences later. And I'm not doing it because Zana thinks I'm a coward. Almost as a joke, I add, "Leave Reverend Bob at home."

"You sure?" asks Julian. "I could make up some judge robes for him, turn him into Judge Bob. He could help with the rulings."

I hope he's kidding.

In the morning, I get the impression that my parents want to ask me if I'm going to the courthouse, if I'm going to follow their wishes or go out on my own. But they don't ask me, and I don't volunteer. I appreciate that they don't press it. I'm sixteen. They leave some things to me.

Julian has borrowed his mother's car. The courthouse is a pain to get to using public transportation. We meet by the bike racks at the school. I tell myself it's because this location is central, but really, I know it would have been just as easy for Julian to pick me up at my house. Why add fuel to the fire, though?

"I'm glad we're going," he says. "The other defendants had a lot of people at their appearances because their names are in the newspapers."

Azeem is a young offender. We know who he is, but most people don't, because his name or anything else that can be used to identify him has to stay out of the media.

"We can't do much, except maybe tell his folks we care about what happens to him. And if he sees a couple of ordinary faces, it might make things easier when he comes back to school."

"You think he's coming back?" I ask. "The police say they have evidence. They say that he attended a terrorist training camp in the woods north of the city."

"Going into the woods doesn't make someone a terrorist," Julian says. "*We* go into the woods!"

"Hey! Slow down!" I put my hand on my friend's arm. Julian tends to drive too fast when he's angry.

We're still two blocks away from the courthouse when we spot the television trucks. The crowds come next.

"I'd better park here," Julian says, heading into a strip mall. We leave the car there and walk the rest of the way.

I feel like I'm stepping into a movie set, or into a foreign country. Julian and I join a moving line of men and women who would not look out of place in a *National Geographic* photo. The men have long beards. They wear *shalwar kameez* and caps or turbans. Few women have faces showing. I see eyes above black veils. Julian nudges me, and I see several women without even eyes, just a black cloth over where their faces would be.

"Go back to where you came from!" a passing driver yells out his window. A Coke can follows, narrowly missing the head of a small child in one of the faceless women's arms.

"We are citizens!" one of the men yells out, but the car is long gone.

The television people zoom in on this, getting reaction, capturing the drama for the evening news.

Julian pushes me through an opening he sees in the crowd. "Let's try to get in and get seats," he says. "I didn't expect all these people."

We have to pass through a metal detector. Our jackets are searched, our ID is checked. The security guards take much more time with me than they do with Julian. He laughs at this when we are finally through.

"What's so funny?" I ask.

"They're more afraid of you than they are of me!" he says. "For a change, I'm the one they *don't* suspect!"

The courtroom quickly fills up. I see two people in the front row. I wonder if they're Azeem's parents. They look sad and scared. I imagine my own parents sitting there.

"Save my seat," I say to Julian, which isn't at all necessary. I slide past people's knees and go up to the man and woman on the front bench. They are dressed like my parents would dress, although the woman has her head covered.

"Are you Azeem's parents?" They nod. I introduce myself. "I do *Reach for the Top* with Azeem. He's very smart."

They nod and thank me for coming. Their eyes are no less sad, but what did I expect? That I'd say something kind about their son and their pain would go away? I go back to Julian.

The bailiff comes in. "All rise."

The judge comes in and sits behind the desk. A lot of legal things are said, which I don't pay attention to. Then Azeem is brought in.

He looks small in his orange jail clothes, and scared. I wonder if the handcuffs are heavy on his wrists. A guard unlocks them and he is told to sit. There is a sheet of glass in front of his bench. I assume it's bulletproof.

The legal talk starts again. Azeem is focused on his parents, but their pain becomes too hard for him to see. He scans the courtroom. I watch his face. He nods slightly, now and then, when he sees someone he knows.

Then his eyes find Julian and me. He actually smiles, and raises his arm in a little wave. We wave back—me timidly, Julian bravely, with a big grin as well.

Heads turn to look at us.

The legal talk takes over. I hear the word *remanded*, the gavel comes down, and Azeem is gone again. It couldn't have taken more than fifteen minutes.

I hear his mother and father crying. Some spectators shout as they are ushered from the courtroom. Soon, Julian and I are back outside.

We're barely out the door when a camera and microphone are stuck in front of us.

"Are you friends of the defendant?"

"We go to the same school," I say, taken by surprise. "We're in the *Reach for the Top* Club."

"Did you have any idea your classmate was involved in terrorist activities?"

"Do you have ESP?" Julian asked back. "Do you have special powers that let you know the outcome of a trial before it even starts? If not, then don't ask such stupid questions."

The camera and the microphone disappear.

Julian laughs. "That will guarantee we don't get on the news! No need to worry about our parents finding out!"

"So you'd begin the Holy Month of Ramadan with a lie?"

I am startled to hear my sister's voice. I look around for her, but all I see is a woman in a black *abaya*, with only her eyes showing.

I know those eyes, though. They are my eyes. Zana and I have the same eyes. It's the only thing about us that's identical. It's eerie, seeing those eyes glaring at me from the top of a black veil.

"Mom and Dad are going to have a fit," I say.

She turns around and walks away.

I shout after her the only thing I can think of, and of course it's something that makes me look like a complete idiot.

"You love music videos just as much as I do!"

What makes it even worse is that she's merged in with a group of other black-clad women. From the back, I can't tell which one is my sister. I may have just yelled at a complete stranger.

Chapter Ten

JAY

SUPPER WAS COOKING AWAY in the kitchen. It smelled good, but after a really tough practice, I wasn't ready to think about food for a little while. I slumped down on the couch and switched on the news. It was just about time. I flicked through the channels and came to a news station. They were reporting on the war in the Middle East. There was always a war in the Middle East.

"How was school today?" my mother yelled from the kitchen.

"Not bad. Hard practice after school."

"I'm afraid I can't come to your game this week!" she called out. "I'm really sorry about that!"

I wasn't. It was nice that my parents were interested but it was a little embarrassing to have your mommy come to all your games.

"That's okay. It's an away game anyway," I called back. "Besides, it's not going to be much of a game."

She came out of the kitchen wiping her hands on her apron. "Any game my son is playing in is an important game. Was there any more news about that student arrested at your school?"

"They're not saying anything. I was hoping to see if there's anything on the news about it," I said.

Right on cue, the news came on back and the announcer started to talk about "homegrown terrorists." The scene shifted to a scene of a big crowd in front of a building.

"That's the courthouse in Brampton," my mother said.

I looked at her curiously. "You been arrested lately?"

"Don't be silly. Jury duty. Turn it up."

I adjusted the volume.

"The juvenile member of the alleged terrorist cell was formally arraigned for bail in Brampton Court today," the announcer said. "The scene was near chaos as family and friends of the accused appeared in court."

It did look like chaos. There were lots of people, lots of brown-skinned men with beards, and lots of women with scarves and veils. A couple of the women wore the entire outfit so you could only see their eyes peeking through layers of black cloth. They looked like characters out of a *Star Wars* sequel—evil characters all dressed in black, probably breathing like Darth Vader.

The announcer went on about all the things I already knew. They talked about the suspect being a Canadian citizen, about more possible arrests. But nothing new.

"Some of the family and friends were interviewed at court," the announcer said and the scene shifted again.

"Are you friends of the defendant?" an unseen voice asked as the camera was shoved into the face of two guys about my age?one black and the other brown. One of them was Haroon, the kid in my geography class.

"We go to the same school," Haroon said. "We're in the *Reach for the Top* Club."

What the hell was a *Reach for the Top* club?

"Did you have any idea your classmate was involved in terrorist activities?" the interviewer asked.

"Do you have ESP?" the black guy shot back. "Do you have special powers that let you know the outcome of a trial before it even starts? If not, then don't ask such stupid questions!"

I laughed out loud.

The scene shifted back to the anchorman, who started to talk about new tax increases. I clicked off the TV and got up off the couch. I needed to eat.

CHAPTER ELEVEN

HAROON

IT IS THE END OF A LONG SCHOOL DAY, nearly two and a half weeks into Ramadan. It's been a strange time, a mixture of prayer and argument. Family and conflict.

My parents see Julian and me on the news, of course. I would have told them anyway. I'm too old to lie to them.

My father turns off the television after my appearance. "You went against our wishes," he says.

It is on the tip of my tongue to say, "It was Julian's idea," but that's a little kid's response. I also think about telling on Zana, but that seems neither mature nor helpful.

"He was glad to see us," I say. "He looked scared. And his parents..." I can't really describe the devastation in his parents' faces. Some of it must show in my own. My parents change their tone.

"We must invite them to *iftar*," my mother says.

They both embrace me long and hard before I go up to bed. I think that is the end of the matter, but my father sticks his head in my bedroom door.

"You will apologize tomorrow to the teachers whose classes you skipped," he says, "and the garage needs cleaning."

At school, Julian's performance on the news makes him a temporary hero and takes any attention off me. Going unnoticed is my usual state, anyway. It's an easy role to slip back into.

The evening of the bail hearing, Zana comes home wearing her usual jeans and sweatshirt. I figure the *abaya* was just another one of those notions she picks up and discards, like the way she leaves her sports stuff all over the house.

I am wrong. A week or so later, she puts it on again. She wears it into the living room, where we are all gathered to break the fast.

My parents look up and their jaws drop.

My mother is the first to speak.

"Are you rehearsing for a play?" Mom asks. "Are you trying out costumes for Halloween? Have you been hit on the head and transported back in time?"

"I kind of like it," Zana says. "Would you rather I dressed like a harlot?"

"Are you saying your mother dresses like a harlot?" Nothing brings out the fire in my father like someone attacking my mother. He goes from mild-mannered literature professor to some kind of creature with claws. It upsets the balance that is him. He never fights for himself that way. Only for us.

"Dressing like this is an expression of piety," Zana says.

I have to laugh out loud at that one. In the last few years, Zana has tried out her "piety" by eating bacon, drinking a wine cooler at a sleepover, and announcing that she wanted to become a Catholic nun. Notions. She drops them as quickly as she picks them up.

"I don't think it would hurt any of us to look more like Muslims," she says.

"Look like Muslims?" My mother pulls her over to the mirror in the hallway and stands there with her. "And how should a Muslim look? There are close to a billion and a half Muslims in the world. Should we all look the same? Should we wear yellow stars, maybe, so we can be easily identified?"

"I'm just saying—"

"You're not saying anything! I've taken you to International Women's Day. We've marched in Take Back the Night. We are feminists!" My mother is really angry. My father and I can only stand out of the way.

"We can wear the *abaya* and still be feminists," my sister begins.

"Women in my family threw off the veil in the 1920s in Afghanistan. Why did they do that? Why did they pay the price of beatings and trouble, just so their great-great-granddaughter could cover herself up like the chattel of some overbearing man?"

"You don't understand."

"No. *You* don't understand. *This* is not Islam! The Koran tells us to be modest, not to disappear!"

"Your interpretation of the Holy Koran is not the only one."

What has begun as a Zana notion, something she might have dropped by the next day, has turned into something much bigger. Nothing brings out her stubbornness like my mother's opposition. I am getting a bad feeling. Neither Zana nor my mother likes to lose an argument, especially not to each other.

"Take it off," my mother says. "Give it back to whatever so-called friends gave it to you. Or better yet, burn it."

"You can't forbid me to wear a religious garment!"

"You are my daughter. I can forbid you from breathing." Which, of course, was completely contrary to everything she'd been saying about women's rights. Mom being sarcastic and irrational is a very dangerous sign.

"It's almost sundown," I say. While my mother and sister glare at each other, I scurry around gathering things together for the start of *iftar*. My father helps, and we are ready in time. Our prayers bring a bit of calm to the house, and my mother and sister declare a truce for the rest of the evening.

Just before I go to bed, Zana comes up to me and says, "You could have backed me up. You could have taken my side."

"What side?" I ask. "I don't know what you're doing."

"I'm your sister," she says. "You shouldn't need to know anything else."

I envy how sure she is of herself.

In the morning, Mom forbids Zana to wear her new clothes to school, but Zana digs her heels in. I don't really think she is ready to appear that way in class, but she's too crazy-stubborn to back down.

"Just wear the *hijab*, then," Mom pleads. "Just cover your head and shoulders. Allow your body to move freely. Allow your pretty face to show to the sun."

But the pleading does no good. At school, Zana folds herself into the group of girls who also wear *abaya*, and I have a hard time picking her out of the crowd.

I try talking to her about it. Well, to be honest, I try ridiculing her about it. She won't talk to me, and she won't fight me. Those folds of black cloth have made her a stranger. At school, I find myself looking at the other kids who wear religious dress, and I blame them for the loss of my sister. I flirt with the idea of turning them all in to the police. I could do it too, even with no evidence. The police would make their lives miserable. But I don't, of course. I don't do anything. I watch Zana's *abaya* flap in the wind, like the wings of a giant crow, as she walks away from me.

I don't even have the guts to tell her that I miss her.

Chapter Twelve
JAY

I SHIFTED ALONG THE LINE. I was moving toward the spot where their quarterback was looking. That was the key: watch the eyes of the quarterback to figure out where you should be. It was an obvious passing situation—last down and twelve to go—so I was going to drop back into coverage and not worry about the run.

Actually, I wasn't going to worry about anything. There were less than two minutes to go and we were up eighty-four to ten. I'd never been in a blowout like this before. And here was a question—why were the starters still out? This was ridiculous, playing us during garbage time. Give the second stringers some playtime and let the rest of us rest and not risk getting injuries. This was stupid. I wasn't sure if Coach was trying to punish the other team or us for not playing hard enough last game. Either way, it was stupid, and I was angry about still being in the game.

Their quarterback called out the signals and I started in toward the line, faking a blitz. As the ball was snapped, I backpedaled until I reached the space by the sideline where he'd been staring. A running back slipped out of the backfield, through our linemen, and into the flat.

I slowed down slightly. I didn't want to rush the play; I wanted the quarterback to think he was open. The running back stopped and turned around, and the ball came floating through the air toward him. I had to time this right. The pass was soft, wobbling, and high. He jumped up into the air to make the catch and just as the ball reached his fingers, I leaped up into the air and drove into him!

He groaned as he was propelled backward, my arms around him, the ball popping loose. He smashed into the ground with me on top of him. I felt his body compress under our combined weight, and he sunk into the turf.

There was a split second of silence. Then the crowd exploded.

"Nice try," I said. I pushed off against the ground and got up. My teammates mobbed me and the crowd continued to yell. I offered him a hand to get up. He just lay there, not moving.

The ref blew his whistle and signaled for their bench to send somebody out. He was hurt. He lay there on the ground, still, not moving. And then he moved…thank goodness he moved… He was okay. He rolled onto his side. He curled his legs up, like he was in pain, and he held his one arm tightly against his body. He was hurt...maybe something was broken.

I didn't mean to hurt him, just hit him.

Suddenly I was pushed sideways by a two-handed shove. One of their players hit me.

"You jerk!" he yelled at me. He was so mad he was practically spitting at me through his face guard. "That was a cheap hit—"

Two of our players knocked him over.

Before I could even think to react, another one of their players started shoving. All four refs came running over and tried to separate everybody. The refs blew their whistles like crazy and grabbed players by their jerseys to pull them apart.

I just stood there, staring, taking in everything. I hadn't done anything wrong. It was a fair hit; he had the ball. It wasn't whistled down by the refs as a penalty.

Slowly the kid got to his feet, supported by one of the coaches. He was holding his one arm with the other. It looked like a collarbone had snapped.

"It was a good hit," one of my players yelled. "Clean hit!"

The refs called a timeout and Coach signaled for some changes. He took me off. I was glad to be finally gone, but part of me wanted to stay on. If somebody else wanted to make something of this, I didn't want them to think I was running.

— ✳ —

At the end of the game as we walked down the line, shaking hands, I heard some grumbling about our team being bad sports, bad winners. I waited for somebody to say something about my hit, but nobody did.

When I passed by the kid I'd hurt, I told him I hoped he'd be okay soon. He told me it was a clean hit—that showed class.

Much more class than their coach. He had words with our coach after the game. I understood why they were upset. It hadn't felt good putting such a beating on them, but we did what we had to do. Besides, it sure beat the heck out of being a bad loser. If they were big enough to play, they were big enough to swallow a loss, no matter how bad.

Just suck it up, take it like a man, shake hands, and leave the field.

The crowd wasn't as big as we usually had for our home games. I guess I couldn't blame them for not showing up. Nobody liked to support a loser.

The Streetsville crowd wasn't much better at losing than their team. And while some of them had left long before the end of the game, the ones who remained yelled out things to us as we passed through the stands toward the dressing room. A couple of those comments were aimed at me. This was one time when keeping my helmet on was a real benefit. It muffled the yelling and protected my head in case somebody threw something down on us as we left the field. As it was, nothing happened.

Nobody seemed to want to leave the locker room. The time right after a big victory was even better than the game itself. Not that it had been much of a game—that one was over before it even began. The only question had been how badly we were going to beat them.

"Can I have your attention for a minute, please?" Coach Pruit called out.

The noise quickly subsided to silence. A couple of guys came out of the shower wrapped only in towels. Everybody else—dressed, half dressed, or still in full uniform—sat or stood, and waited.

"Today was a glorious day...if you were wearing a *Central* uniform."

There was a smattering of laughter and cheering.

"We did what we needed to do. Despite what *some* people might say." We all knew he was referring to the Streetsville coach. "We did what we had to do. Losing wasn't an option. That was a war out there, a battle, and while we don't necessarily enjoy crushing somebody into the ground—"

"I liked watching Jay do it, though!" somebody yelled from the back and everybody laughed.

"Sometimes it is good," Coach Pruit said. "It was a good hit. If they wanted to be angry at anybody, it should have been at their quarterback for throwing up such a lame-duck pass."

"They always blame the quarterback!" Kevin yelled out.

"All the glory and all the blame all the time," Steve announced.

"Anyway," Coach Pruit continued, "I know it's better to crush somebody than to be crushed. The lessons you learn in football are the lessons you learn for life. I remember one of my coaches telling me that you learn more from losing than you do from winning. So I guess our opponents should be thanking us for the education we gave them today."

There was more laughter and comments.

"Today we gave them all a collective PhD. And when those ratings come out next week, you can count on us not being ranked fifth, or fourth, or even third. You can even count on us not being ranked second, because second is not an option. We will be ranked where we belong. Number one!"

Almost in unison, everybody started cheering, "We're number one! We're number one!" The noise kept building and building and building, until it wasn't just something coming out of my lungs or into my ears but filled every part of my body.

We *were* number one.

— ✳ —

I waited impatiently for the last few players to leave the locker room. Kevin had to be last, Steve before him, then me. It was one of those unwritten rules like finishing first when doing laps or wind sprints, or keeping your helmet on while the coach was talking. Those were things the captain did. Things I'd do next year and teach the guy who would be captain the year after me.

"Come on, Moose!" Kevin yelled. "Hurry up or you'll miss the bus!"

"Keep your shirt on," Moose replied.

"We have *our* shirts on. Get a move on!"

Slowly Moose stood up, pulled on his shirt, and grabbed his equipment bag. He took a few steps and staggered, almost falling down.

Steve grabbed Moose by the arm and helped him to the bench.

"You okay?" Kevin asked anxiously, as he stood over top of him.

"Yeah...just got a little lightheaded... That's all."

"It looked like you were going to faint."

"I'm okay."

"Jay, get him something to drink, some Gatorade," Kevin ordered.

"No," Moose said abruptly. "Nothing to drink. I can't have anything to drink. Ramadan."

"Ramadan?" Steve asked. "Is that like diabetes or something?"

Kevin shook his head. "Steve, sometimes you amaze me."

"Sometimes I amaze me too, but what's that got to do with diabetes?"

"Ramadan is a special time in the Muslim calendar," Moose said. "For a month we have to be more observant of our faith."

"What's that got to do with you almost fainting?" Steve asked.

"For the whole month we can't drink or eat—"

"You can't eat for a month? That's impossible!" Steve said. "I can hardly survive until fourth period for lunch!"

"No, no, we eat and drink, we just can't do either between sunrise and sunset," Moose explained.

"For the whole month?" Steve said, repeating it like he really didn't believe his ears.

Moose nodded. "We eat a big meal for breakfast with lots to drink. Then we fast all day until we have another big meal as soon as the sun sets."

"No wonder you almost fainted," Kevin said. "You can't play a football game without drinking something."

"You can. I have. This is week three of Ramadan and my third game."

"What happened today?"

"I slept in this morning and didn't have a chance to drink enough before the sun came up. It was hot today and Coach Pruit played me into the fourth quarter."

"Why didn't you tell him to take you out?" I asked.

"I couldn't. I didn't tell him about any of this. I was afraid he wouldn't play me at all." He paused. "You guys aren't going to tell him, are you?"

We waited for Kevin to answer. Whatever he said, we'd go along with it. It was much easier than actually having to form our own opinion.

"Just one more week, right?" Kevin asked.

"One more."

"And you'll drink and eat more before that game and the rest of the practices, right?"

"I won't make that mistake again," Moose said reassuringly.

"We're a better team with you on the field than off," Kevin said. "This stays in the locker room, okay?" he asked, turning toward me and Steve.

I nodded. "Count on it."

"No question," Steve said.

"Then come on. Let's get going."

Moose got up and Steve took his one arm.

"Carry his bag," Kevin ordered. "You two stay close to him on the bus and I'll drive him straight home from school."

— ✳ —

137

We had been the last on the bus, and we needed to be the last off. We wanted to wait until Coach Pruit and the other three assistants were inside the school in case Moose had another little stumble. It was also better that nobody else on the team saw it either.

"How you feeling?" I asked Moose.

"I'm feeling okay. Just really hungry and thirsty. What time is it?"

"Almost six."

"Then I don't have to wait very long. Sunset is at 6:25 today."

"That early? Are you sure?" Steve asked.

"Believe me, if you were fasting all day you'd know exactly when sunset happens."

"We'll have you home by then," Kevin said. "Let's go."

We got up and walked off the bus. All three of us watched him pretty carefully.

"I'm just parked over here," Kevin offered.

"I have to go to my locker," Moose said. "Homework."

"Forget the homework," Steve said.

"Can't. I have a calculus test tomorrow. I need my book."

"Forget it. So you get an eighty instead of a ninety. Big deal."

"It's more like a forty instead of a sixty. I need to pass to stay on the team."

"I thought all brown people did well in math," Steve said.

"That's Chinese people," Moose said.

"Most of the brown people in my classes do pretty good."

"Not all. It's a stereotype," Moose said. "Sort of like all black people can dance."

"That one's true," Steve joked.

"Yeah, right," Kevin said. "Obviously you've never seen yourself on video."

"Look who's talking! I can bust a move and you look like all of your moves are busted!"

"I need my textbooks," Moose said again.

"Fine, we'll get you your textbooks." Kevin shook his head slowly. "Anybody else need to get something from their locker?"

"Yeah, right. Like I'm going to study," Steve snorted.

"Me neither."

"Good. You two walk him to his locker and I'll pull the car around the back and meet you there."

We started for the school while Kevin went for the car. Moose was moving slowly but he seemed pretty solid on his feet. We entered the school. It was, once again, that quiet time I liked so much. The school was deserted. Some of the lights were out, making the halls dim. We headed toward the shop classes. Moose's locker was, of course, in the brown corridor. I was grateful for that. The rest of us had lockers by the gym, close to the gym office. The coaches usually stayed there after every game, going over film. Moose's locker was nowhere near them.

We passed by Azeem's gaping locker. The police tape might have been gone, but the missing door pretty well marked the spot. I wondered if they'd found anything in it. If they had, we probably would have heard about it on the news. That was the only way we would have heard about it. Still nothing from the school.

"Here it is," Moose said.

"How come you're having trouble in calculus?" Steve asked.

"My parents think it's because I'm wasting too much time playing football," he said as he removed a book.

"Playing football isn't wasting time," Steve said firmly.

"Tell that to my parents. They think that anything under a ninety is a disgrace to the family."

"If I pulled off a ninety, my parents wouldn't know whether to throw me a party or have me tested for performance-enhancing drugs."

"Maybe they'd do both," I suggested.

Moose slammed his locker closed and clicked the lock back on. We went down the corridor toward the back doors where Kevin would be waiting.

"A Big Mac," Steve said. "No, make that *two* Big Macs."

"What about two Big Macs?" I asked.

"That's the first thing I'd eat if I hadn't eaten all day. Two Big Macs, a big order of fries, and the biggest Coke they have."

"The Coke and fries sound good, but I don't eat meat," Moose said.

"You're a vegetarian?" I asked.

"Normally I eat some meat, but none during the holy seasons like Ramadan."

We opened the door and took two steps before we skidded to a stop.

Standing in the middle of Brown Town were Mr. Atkins, one of the vice-principals, a couple of teachers, some kids, one of the caretakers and two cops. For a second I thought about turning us around and heading back into the school. But the principal saw us and motioned for us to join them.

CHAPTER THIRTEEN

HAROON

I WALK MS. SINGH to her car after our late *Reach for the Top* practice.

"Less than two weeks left before the show," she says. "Ramadan will be over, and there will be nutrition as well as brilliance flowing through your brains."

Does she ever get tired? She bounces with every step, just like she does in the first class of the morning. Even when it isn't Ramadan, I'm often wiped by the end of the day.

We leave the nearly empty school together and cross the lawn, heading to the teachers' parking lot. We see a few kids standing on the edge of Brown Town, looking down at something.

"What's going on?" Ms. Singh wonders. We walk over there to find out.

"They wonder how 9/11 could have happened," I hear someone say as we get closer. "They wonder why we are angry."

And then I see.

The lawn and benches of Brown Town, the place

where Muslim students gather every day to talk, to pray, to just be with others who have things in common, is now defiled. Racial slurs are painted on the benches. The ground is covered with pieces of something that is sort of light brown and sort of pink. It takes me a moment to identify it.

It is ham.

CHAPTER FOURTEEN

JAY

BY THE TIME we got to Brown Town, the principal and the caretaker had joined the other kids. We stumbled forward, stopping just on the outside of the small circle of people. Now it was obvious why they were there. The walls of the school, the concrete, and the benches were all covered with orange spray paint. There were crude letters, quickly drawn words. Over the bike racks, it read Camel Parking. Two of the benches had the words Sand Monkey Seating on them. There were other words, words I couldn't read. And there was something all over the concrete, all over the ground. Sort of pink confetti or ribbons or—

"Is that ham?" Steve asked. He looked stunned.

"Yes, it is," Mr. Atkins said.

"But why would anybody throw ham around?" I questioned.

"Pork is the most impure meat," Moose said. "It's an insult against Muslims, just like the words."

"But...but...who would do this?" I stammered. I looked up at the others. One of them was Haroon, the one who'd been handcuffed by mistake.

144

"We have no idea. We're hoping somebody will come forward with some information," Mr. Atkins said.

"We weren't even here," Steve protested. "We were at the football game against Streetsville. We won the game. Right, Moose?" Steve sounded guilty, speaking up like that.

"Yeah. We won," Moose agreed.

"Somebody will know," our principal said. "This isn't the work of just one person, so it won't stay a secret."

"Don't you have a camera aimed at this area?" I asked, looking around for one.

"None here, but we'll find out."

I heard the roar of an engine and looked up expecting to see Kevin's car. Instead, a news truck squealed to a halt.

"How did they find out?"

"Nothing stays a secret," Ms. Singh, one of the teachers, said. There was more than a hint of sarcasm in her voice.

"We don't need any more bad publicity," Mr. Atkins said. He turned to the police officers. "Can you keep them away for a few minutes?"

One of the officers had stripes on his epaulets—a sergeant. "A couple of minutes. Why?"

"I was just hoping we could clean it up a little before they start taking pictures. We can clean it up now, right?"

"We have our evidence," the sergeant said. The other officer held up a camera.

"Good. Thanks. If you can just get us a few minutes, we'd really appreciate it. We don't want this thing blown out of proportion."

"Neither do we," the sergeant said. "The less publicity this generates the better."

They went over to intercept the two men who had gotten out of the news truck.

"Could everybody please gather around," our principal said.

We all moved a little bit closer, but nobody seemed to want to get too close.

"The arrest of one of our students has caused a great deal of suffering here at the school," he said.

"Not to mention the suffering it has caused the student and his family," Ms. Singh said.

He looked at her, furrowed his brow slightly, and then continued. "The last thing we need is publicity."

"Are you suggesting keeping the press out?" Ms. Singh asked angrily. "Freedom of the press is one of the foundations of democracy."

Mr. Atkins glowered at her. "Thank you for the grade-nine civics lesson, Ms. Singh," he snapped. "I am suggesting that this message of hatred and intolerance can only lead to further hatred and intolerance, inflaming emotions and actions on both sides. There is no need for the world to see these words.

They need to see the actions of our students and staff to fix what has been done. Does anybody disagree?" he demanded.

I assumed it was a rhetorical question. Adults always ask questions they don't want answered.

"Raise your hand if you'd like to do something about this."

There seemed no choice but to raise our hands, which we all did.

"Excellent. Right here, right now, we're going to work as a team to clean this mess up. If the media has to see these words, they are also going to see our students work together to erase those words."

"I'll help, for sure," Steve said, "but I'm a little worried about Moose here. He's not feeling well. Kevin's going to drive him home." He gestured and we all turned around. Kevin, along with the two news people, was standing behind the two officers who blocked them from moving closer.

"I'm okay," Moose said.

"You look awful," Ms. Singh said. "Are you fasting and playing football?"

That was the last thing we wanted anybody to ask.

"I'm okay," he repeated without either answering her question or lying.

"Fine, Moose. Kevin can take you home. Can I count on the rest of you?" Mr. Atkins looked at us.

Again, what choice did we have but to nod our heads in agreement?

"Mr. Caldwell," the principal said, "Let one of the students use the broom. Another can have the dustpan. Do you think the paint can be washed away with soapy water and a scrub brush?"

"It's still fresh. Some of it, depending on the type of paint."

"And the words that can't be removed?"

"Can be covered up with spray paint," Mr. Caldwell offered.

"Excellent. If you could get these supplies, we will all get to work."

— ✳ —

Steve and I both used scrub brushes to try to remove the paint. It was hard work, and after a while I could feel it in my arms, but it seemed to be working. There were still bits of orange paint showing on the benches, but it was impossible to read the words. The concrete walls were bumpy and rough and the paint had gotten itself into the bumps so much that it was almost impossible to get out. Mr. Caldwell used the gray spray paint to simply cover up the whole area. That worked well, although in some ways it just made for a nice clean canvas for the next set of people with a spray can. Hopefully that wouldn't be the case here.

I looked slightly over my shoulder. The camera was aimed at the two of us. I looked away. I had been really aware of the camera for the first ten or fifteen minutes, and then my attention had sort of faded. The news guys had wanted to interview us about what had happened and what we were doing, but our principal wouldn't let them. He said that without our parents giving written permission, he couldn't allow that to take place on school property. Instead, they just shot the whole thing, the camera panning around.

Steve stood up, turned around, and faced the camera with a big smile on his face. Steve had worked hard to make sure he was in a whole lot of the shots.

"Hey. I know you," Steve said.

I looked over. He was talking to Haroon.

"You're a friend of Julian's," Steve added.

The kid nodded. "Yes."

"I'm Steve Morgan."

"I know."

"You do... Have we met?"

The kid shrugged. "You're on the football team. Everybody knows the guys on the football team. I'm Haroon."

"Good to meet you. Any friend of Julian's is a friend of mine."

The two of them shook hands.

149

"And since you know me, you must know Jay."

I stood up and we shook hands. "I know you too," I said. "You're in my geography class. And I saw you on TV from the court."

He looked surprised and then embarrassed. "Unfortunately, you weren't the only one. Julian thought it was a joke. My parents didn't think it was so funny. They really didn't like me being at court."

"Why did you go?" Steve asked.

"I guess we were just sort of curious. Plus we wanted to show support for Azeem."

"So you knew him," Steve said.

"Did the team win by a lot?" Haroon asked, abruptly changing the subject. Obviously, he didn't want to talk about that anymore.

"Yeah. Easy win," I answered. "Why were you still here?"

"Practice."

"What team?" Volleyball would be starting up soon.

"We're on the *Reach for the Top* team."

"The what?" Steve asked.

He'd mentioned that on the news. The terrorist kid was on it too.

"*Reach for the Top*. Our school has a team in the contest. We give answers to questions. It's a TV show."

"Yeah, yeah. I know that show," Steve said.

"Do you watch it?" Haroon asked. He sounded hopeful.

Steve shook his head. "Nope."

"I didn't know we had a team like that," I said.

"I don't think many people know. Azeem was on the team. They arrested him during practice."

"That would have been pretty exciting," Steve said.

"Not the word I'd use."

I had to agree with him there.

"I guess you're getting to be a real TV star," Steve said. "That *Reach for the Top* thing. You were on the news the other day, and we're definitely on tonight's news. Smile for the camera."

CHAPTER FIFTEEN

HAROON

A SPECIAL ASSEMBLY is called the next morning, taking us out of our classes. I've never seen the principal so angry. He rages against the vandals and threatens dire consequences for anyone who even thinks of pulling a similar stunt, in the school or in the community.

We file back to class. I hear phrases in the hall like "Troublemakers," "Probably did it themselves," and "They'll never catch the guys," and "Surveillance cameras all over the school."

I realize I am surrounded by kids who are not Muslim. I start to feel scared until I spot another Muslim student. I've never felt that at my school before.

At home, my parents are trying hard to keep a truce between themselves and my sister. We have guests every evening for *iftar*. Hospitality is part of the tradition, but the guests also act as a buffer. Julian joins us one evening. He talks with Zana the same way he would if she were wearing her usual blue jeans and sweatshirt. The normalcy of it calms me down.

"The magic Julian," I tell him. "Thanks."

He gives me his crazy grin and goes off into the night.

I try to get more into the spirit of the holiday by reading one of the books I've had since I was a kid. It's on the life of the Prophet. The story is so wonderful and familiar that it calms me too. I begin to think that this Ramadan might turn out all right after all.

Then the phone rings.

Thinking it's Julian, I pick up the receiver.

"Hello?"

An operator speaks. "I have a collect call here for Haroon Badawi from Azeem. Will you accept the charges?"

I am stunned. "Yes," I say. The operator goes off the line and Azeem comes on.

"Hello? Haroon?"

"Yes. It's me. Hello."

"Thank you for taking my call. They only let you make collect calls from here."

"Are you still in jail?" It's a stupid question to ask, but sometimes stupid questions are comforting. You both know they're stupid, but you also both know you'll get through it.

"I don't like it much," he says.

"I wouldn't, either."

"It was good to see you in court the other day. You and Julian. Please tell him I said so."

"I will. We were glad to come. Well, not glad."

"I know what you mean. It's okay. A lot of kids I thought were my friends won't take my calls. They have me in a cell by myself. All I talk to all day is adults, and you know how tiring that can be."

I laugh. "I know. You can never be yourself around adults."

"Haroon?" he says. "I would like to wish you and your family a Happy Ramadan."

"Thank you," I say. "The same to you. Are you able to observe?"

"They're very careful about that," he says. "They make sure I have the right food and everything, but it's not the same as being at home."

"My parents are going to invite your parents to *iftar*," I tell him.

"They're taking this pretty hard."

I don't want to tell him, but I have to. "I have your spot on the team."

"I know," he says. "And I know you didn't turn me in to the police to get it."

I'm surprised he's heard, but rumors do have a way of getting around.

"You're better than me in geography, but you're not as good as I am on the mathematics questions," he says.

"I know," I say. "I'm working on it, but I don't have the same kind of mind as you. I'd get my sister to help me, but we're not getting along right now."

"It's Ramadan. It's the time to make peace."

"I'm working on it," I say again.

"I could coach you," he offers. "On the math, not your sister."

I'm surprised that he's able to make a joke. "That would be helpful," I say. "Thank you."

"I have to go," he says. "Can I call you again?"

"Anytime," I tell him. And then he is gone.

Another toss and turn night. I finally get to sleep. Moments later, my father is knocking at my door, waking me up for *sohour*. I try to embrace the day with a good spirit. It isn't easy.

The news continues to be filled with threats. I take to buying newspapers on the way to school. There are photos of stranded passengers flooding airports and pictures of British Muslims arrested for alleged plots to blow things up in England. There are stories and maps showing the places in my city that are most vulnerable to terrorists. When I walk down the street, white people look at me in fear, even though I am dressed like they are dressed. Even though my national anthem is the same as theirs.

"We need to re-examine our immigration policy," news commentators say. "Why are these people being allowed into our country?" When it's pointed out that many of those arrested were actually born here and are citizens, the commentators and columnists say, "The Muslim community must take responsibility for extremism in their midst."

The newspapers are also full of shattered buildings in Iraq and dead civilians in Afghanistan.

"If they stop killing us over there, we'll stop killing them here," says Hadi, whose locker is next to mine.

"Nobody's killing you," I say. "Get your own paper." He flicks his fingers at the headlines and leaves me alone.

Azeem calls a couple more times. I tell no one about his calls. I try to get to the phone first when it rings, just in case it's him. We don't talk for long. He probably has limits on how long he can use the phone. He doesn't talk about what it's like in jail, and I don't ask him if he's guilty. We talk a bit about school, but mostly he gives me math tips. He says it is a distraction for him to work out shortcuts to give to me. His shortcuts work. They don't work as well for me as they do for him, because I simply don't have a math brain, but my time and success rate on those questions during drills improves. Ms. Singh even pauses one day during the rapid-fire section to say, "Well done," which almost never happens.

Azeem's parents come to *iftar*, but it is not a successful evening. They don't want to ruin our Ramadan with talk of their sorrow, and we don't know them well enough to talk about anything else. We should have invited Julian as well.

Things are quieter at home, but not calmer. My parents will not reconcile themselves to my sister wearing full veil. They refuse to speak about it, as a concession to the spirit of Ramadan. But their silence is a loud, resentful one. And Zana, stubborn mule that she is, makes it even worse. She brings home a *hijab* for my mother and leaves it on the kitchen table with my mother's name on it. I hear my mother and father arguing about it, trying to keep their words quiet. In the morning, the *hijab* is gone, replaced by more silence.

"What's gotten into you?" I ask Zana one afternoon after school. She is preparing to go to her friend's house for *iftar*. Mom is at the hospital. It looks like it will be just Dad and me tonight. "You never cared about religion before. You told me once that the only thing you liked about the holidays was the new clothes."

"I don't expect you to understand," she says, moving to the front door and covering her face as she looks out for her ride. "It's a known fact that women mature faster than men."

That is a wonderfully Zana-like arrogant statement, but I'm not letting her get away with it. "Then explain it to me simply. Because kids are asking me about it at school, and I don't know what to tell them."

That's partly a lie. No one has come right out and

asked, not even Julian, but some have said things to me, as if they already know.

Hadi told me, "It's good that you are finally getting control of your sister."

Girls from Zana's basketball team glared at me in the hallway between classes, and I heard one of them say, "He's the one making her wear that thing!"

It makes me feel guilty, even though both comments are laughable. Nobody can make Zana do something she doesn't want to do—not me, not the government, not even our mother. Have they *met* Zana?

"Tell me," I say again.

Zana sighs then says, "I'll try, but you won't get it. You float through life thinking everything and everyone is wonderful."

That sounds like an insult, but I'm not certain.

"All around the world, we're under attack. It's everywhere you look: Palestine, Iraq, Chechnya, Europe, North America."

"Muslims are not being attacked because of religion," I say. "They—we—they are being attacked because of land and oil."

Zana keeps talking as if I haven't spoken.

"And when a group you belong to is under attack, if you don't show your loyalty, then you're siding with the attackers."

"What kind of logic is that? The world is not us and them! The world is...many shades of all of us!"

"I told you that you wouldn't understand. You're still a child, and you're not ready to hear me."

If we were eight years younger, and this were not Ramadan, I could tackle her and we could wrestle it out on the living room floor. She'd probably win, but at least I'd feel like it was a fair fight.

"What about the Islamic militia killing people in Darfur?" I call after her as she leaves the house. "We are not always on the side of the victims!"

She starts to walk away from me.

"You marched against the Taliban!" I call after her.

I watch Zana get into a car full of women who are veiled the way she is, including the woman who is driving. I want to yell at them. *If this were Saudi Arabia, you wouldn't be allowed to drive!* Luckily, my mouth stays shut, since that would have made about as much sense as the Gwen Stefani remark.

My father will be home from work soon. Mom has left a chicken and rice casserole in the fridge. I put it in the oven and set the table. I am looking forward to a quiet evening. So is my father, judging from the calm expression on his face when he arrives. With both my mother and sister gone, it will be an evening without argument.

After we eat, he suggests going to evening prayers at the mosque.

I'm surprised. It's not unheard of, but it's not usual, either, for us.

"I feel like being out in the world with my son," he says.

We walk the few blocks to the mosque. I see Arab Muslims, Afghan Muslims, Somali Muslims, Muslims from India, and Muslims from Indonesia. Some are in traditional, national dress. Some, like my father and me, are in suits.

As we rise and fall in prayer with the others, Ms. Singh's question comes into my head. Am I praying to a God that created my ancestors, or did my ancestors create the God that I am praying to? Does it even matter? The prayers, the celebration, the joining with others, is beautiful. Does it matter where it all sprang from? Do the two views always have to be at war?

And then I put those thoughts away, and give myself over to the prayers.

The October evening is soft and warm. We stop at an Afghan bakery for some of the honey snacks my father is so fond of and which my mother tries to limit in favor of fruit. "It's a holiday," he says with a smile.

We do not rush on the way home. We don't talk, we just walk. My father, like Julian, also likes companionable silences.

There is a police car waiting outside our house when we turn onto our block. Out comes Detective Moffett and another officer.

"Professor Badawi? Good evening, Haroon."

My father shakes the police officers' hands, and

invites them in for tea and Afghan treats. "It's probably best to have these eaten before my wife gets
home, anyway."

I do not have a good feeling about this. I am sure
they are not here to wish us a Happy Ramadan.

"We are sorry to disturb you, Professor Badawi.
We won't take much of your time. We just wanted to
know if you were aware that your son has been
accepting phone calls from one of the suspected terrorists we have in custody."

I am glad it is my father's steadiness that
responds, not my mother's argumentativeness. I
know he is taken by surprise, but his voice betrays
nothing, not even the slightest quiver.

"I assume you are speaking of the child you have
locked up. He and my son know each other from
school. It's natural that youth seeks out youth."

The cops look at my father silently for a long
moment. I'm getting to know the way they use
silence. I wonder if they come by it naturally or if
they learn it at the police academy.

My father doesn't squirm, or look away, or talk to
fill up the space. He likes silence.

"We have to use all the tools we can to fight this
terrible threat," Detective Moffett says.

"Every tool the law has to offer," my father adds.

"If you can't keep a closer watch on your son,
we'll have to."

"Since you know that he's been receiving the boy's phone calls, you probably also know the content of the calls."

"Prisoners have no expectations of privacy, except when they consult with their lawyers. Your son is not a lawyer."

"My son is also not in prison, but leaving aside his right to privacy for a moment, I would bet you this box of Afghan delicacies that they have talked about no more than school and the other usual things boys have in common. Am I right?" He holds out the box of sweets.

Detective Moffett tries his silence trick again, but not for long. He can see it doesn't work on my father.

"You might want to advise your son not to accept any more calls."

"Thank you for your kind advice," my father says. "I hope you both enjoy the rest of this beautiful evening."

The officers get back in their car and drive away. I stand beside my father by our front door until the police car has gone down the street and we can't hear it or see it anymore.

Then my father says, "Your grandparents left Afghanistan so that we would not be bothered by war, or chaos, or hatred, or suspicion, so we could live our lives without fear or torture or police brutality, or the kind of craziness that plagues most of the people on this sad planet. Our parents worked hard, and we have worked hard, to give you and your sister a decent life, an ideal life. And both of you, each in your own way, have brought the world's craziness right into our house."

He unlocks the front door and goes inside. I stay on the porch, standing alone and looking out at the night.

Chapter Sixteen

HAROON

I'M IN CHARGE OF TAPING.

It's the day before *Eid*. Probably. There's always some discussion about when Ramadan actually ends and *Eid* begins since it depends on the moon instead of a calendar, but it's likely going to be tomorrow. My family has spent the last day of Ramadan working at the food bank for as long as I can remember.

This is the first time I've been assigned the tape dispenser—the one that rolls the wide, clear tape across the open flaps of cardboard, binding them into a box and cutting off the edges, neat and sharp. When I was a little kid, I'd watch the person with taping privileges out of the corner of my eye while I counted out tins of tuna and beans. "Can I have a try?" I always asked, and was always told that I was too small and could hurt myself. I suspected that was a lie at the time, and now that I finally get to tape (I'm both big enough and the only one yet on the task), I know that I was right. Making something solid out of what was moments before useless and flat is very satisfying.

It's the mood I'm in, I think. The food bank is a productive place, where things get done and something gets fixed. Food gets into empty bellies. How much simpler can it get?

Zana is working as far away from me as she can get. She hasn't spoken to me in nearly a week. When she gets mad, she holds onto it.

"Are you going to hog that thing all morning?" Julian asks. He's here with us, of course. He volunteers at a million things but never seems rushed, never seems stressed. He's here because we're here— my family, I mean. He always celebrates *Eid* with us, just as I always celebrate Kwanza with him and his mom.

"I'm not sure you should say the word 'hog' to a Muslim," I answer. "I think that qualifies as an insult, which means I get to keep taping."

You never know where Julian is going to go with something. To pretend to bug me, he goes into a long, fast lecture on pigs, specifically breeds of pigs, and each new breed gets talked about in a different accent.

"The Yorkshire pig is the aristocrat of hogs," he says, in a fair imitation of Prince Charles. "It's the pig that ruled the British Empire, what, what?"

Then he switches to a drawl more Western than Westerners. "The dream of the Chester White is to end up on a Texas barbecue grill, feeding Republicans, making 'em grow up strong."

165

"Where do you keep all that information—in your dreadlocks?" I ask.

He slips back into Jamaican, something about wild pigs on the beach trained to root out tourists who've been buried in the sand. "Tourist-hunting pigs, the cool cousins of the truffle-hunters of France."

I'm laughing so hard that I loosen my grip on the taping machine, and Julian grabs his chance. "Never mind, little boy," he says. "There's always a chance next year."

I'm demoted back to my usual job, packing empty boxes with cheap protein and budget-stretching noodles. I'm glad the food is all nonperishable, packaged up and scentless. There was one year when we volunteered at a hot lunch program at a drop-in center. A major restaurant had donated big trays of lasagna. It smelled so good, and I was so hungry from fasting that it was all I could do to keep myself from plunging my whole face into the fragrant noodles and sauce.

There are many people from my mosque here today. We always have a Ramadan food drive, part of *zakat*, or the right of the needy. Some people are packing up boxes of *halal* food, to deliver to new refugee families from Somalia and the Sudan who couldn't afford to celebrate *Eid* otherwise. Most of the food we collect goes to non-Muslim families. As our imam says, hunger is hunger.

My father is picking up his brother and family from the airport. They're flying in from California to be with us for *Eid*. My cousin Mahmoud is also a runner, and gets along well with Julian. It's going to be a good *Eid*.

My mother and sister are here. My mother is organizing a group of volunteers at the other end of the warehouse.

I look across the warehouse and watch Zana pick up a filled box. She catches her *abaya* on something and trips, spilling the box. A can of pineapple chunks rolls its way over to me. I stop it with my foot and take it to her.

"Are you all right?" I ask.

"*Now* you want to know?"

"I mean, did you hurt yourself when you tripped?" Why does she have to be so touchy all the time?

"I've fallen before." She repacks the box, snatching the can of pineapple from my hand and tucking it next to the peanut butter. She goes to lift the box onto the table, ready for the final taping.

"Let me help you with that," I say.

"I'm stronger than you are." Which is almost true.

I watch her for a moment, as she reaches for another empty box and begins putting groceries into it.

"Why?" I ask her. The word comes out before I even realize I'm going to ask it.

She stops packing. Her eyes, all I can see of her face, look at me over the black veil.

"Why?" I ask again. "Just tell me. You've found God, you're doing it to annoy Mom, you're doing it on a dare or a bet—whatever. Just tell me why. I'm ready to hear you now."

Although I can't see the rest of her face, I can read her eyes. I never realized before how much you can read in just a person's eyes. Always before, I've had the whole face to look at and interpret. But all I have now of my sister is her eyes. And I can tell she's trying to decide whether to bother telling me.

Then she speaks. "Ever since September eleventh—before that, but especially then—people have hated us because we're Muslims—don't interrupt me!"

I have no intention of interrupting. I am too happy to have her actually talking with me.

She continues. "They hate our names, they hate our traditions, and they think we're all mindless terrorists who want to strap dynamite to our chests and go blow up a Toys "R" Us. They don't see us as people."

She pauses. I take a chance on speaking, hoping she doesn't think I'm interrupting. "But if we continue to look and behave so differently from most people," I say, "they'll never trust us."

Zana sits down on a crate of kidney beans. I give

her a moment to work out what she's trying to say. "Not all of us can do that," she tells me. "How we dress is so much a part of who we are. Some women believe—*believe*—it is their duty to God to be fully covered. Some have only been in this country a short while, and they have worn the veil in their home countries all their lives. When they must get used to so many new things already, do we really need to add clothes to that?"

"But people think *I* make you wear this," I say. "They think Dad and I are oppressing you. It's fine if you believe in it, or if you're used to it, but that's not you. Why do *you* have to wear it?"

She stands up and goes back to work, dismissing me. "It's called solidarity, Haroon. Look it up sometime."

I leave her alone. Zana. I'd resent her if I didn't love her so much. All I can do is be proud of her, even when I don't understand her. Even when she drives me up the wall.

"How's the packing going?" Dad asks.

"Dad! You're here early!" The plan was for him to meet us here in a couple of hours, with Uncle Asif and family in tow. We were going to go out to dinner at the Khyber Pass Afghan restaurant. Mom made a reservation. "Where is everybody? Was their plane early?"

"Where's your mother?" Dad asks in return,

which is not a good sign. Bad news gets broken first to Mom, then to us. I nod toward the sorting department at the other end of the warehouse. He heads that way. Zana, Julian, and I go after him. Julian leaves the tape machine behind. I don't know why I care enough to even notice that, when something more important is going on.

"What is it?" Mom asks, seeing Dad's face and stepping her way through the maze of food donations.

"They weren't allowed on the plane," my father says. "They had their tickets, their identification— everything was in order. But my brother's name came up on a no-fly list!"

"What's that?" I ask, although I feel that I should already know.

"It's a list of people the government thinks might be terrorists," one of the sorting volunteers says. "It's a list of people the government says it doesn't trust to get on a plane."

"Uncle Asif?" I ask. "That doesn't make sense." Uncle Asif was born in Sacramento. He owns a string of car dealerships. "He sells Fords!"

It's a ridiculous thing to say, but no one says so or rolls their eyes. The whole situation is ridiculous.

"They've got him mixed up with someone else," my mother says, in that matter-of-fact voice of hers that says this is simply a mess that will be straightened out. "They've got him confused with another man of the same name."

"So someone else should be kept from flying so that your relative can be kept in peace?" the volunteer asks. "Your brother's right to fly is more important than this other person's?"

"They've made a mistake," my mother says firmly. "You think these groceries are going to sort themselves?" She moves my family and Julian over to an empty space, away from prying ears. "I will call someone."

"Who?" my father asks. "In time for *Eid*? Who can be called?"

"I don't know," my mother tells him. "I will call...someone."

My mother is a scientist. She refuses to believe there is such a thing as a problem that has no solution.

My father deals with literature. He knows better.

She hustles us back to work. Julian doesn't even try for the tape machine again. He stays close to me and Zana. We all pack side by side.

"There was a blacklist in the 1950s," he says. This time there is no funny accent. "Your name went on it if someone said you were a communist. Sometimes the committee would make a mistake, put the wrong name on the list. The poor sap would go to them and say, 'You've got the wrong person!' and the committee would say, 'Prove you're not a communist by giving us the names of other communists.' The guy would say, 'But I don't know any communists!' and the committee would say, 'If you won't cooperate with us, you must be a communist.'"

I reach for a can of lentils, and wish Julian would go back to talking about pigs.

— * —

The next day I go to the mosque with my family to celebrate *Eid* with prayers and community. Our imam talks about how faith can be a source of comfort in times of trouble, a pathway to the past and the future. I keep that in mind as I pray beside my father, saying words that have been said for centuries, by people all over the world. I feel my mind touching all those lives, imagining their struggles, their triumphs, and then imagining that, hundreds of years from now, someone will be thinking back to me. For all the things that tear us apart—our human failures of injustice and greed—we are united in the prayers we say and our search for comfort in the endless universe.

I'm feeling calmer than I have in a while as I put on my shoes after the service and walk out into the sunshine with my family.

"There are always problems," I say, walking with them toward the parking lot. "While we're in them, they seem really important, but time goes on and they're just blips. The things that last are not the things we worry about."

My mother puts her arm around my waist. She used to be able to put it around my shoulders, but I've grown so much.

We make slow progress. Many people have come to the mosque today. There are lots of friends to exchange greetings with. Even people we don't know wish us Happy *Eid*, and we return the wishes.

The world and the ugliness it has recently brought to our small piece of it seems far away. The peace of the prayers have even put at bay thoughts of our relatives who were wrongly kept from joining us. I love my family, I love my community, and I just feel good.

Of course, it doesn't last.

There are groups of people in the parking lot, huddled over copies of a newspaper. We are drawn to them by the energy of anger, outrage, and betrayal that hovers over them.

"What have we become?" an old man asks. "How can we stand together when there are those among us who want to rip us apart?"

"What do you expect? There are always people who cause trouble for everyone," a younger man says.

"Cause trouble, or prevent trouble?" another man asks.

"May we see the newspaper?" my father asks. "What is going on?"

The newspaper is passed over to him. I lean in to read with the rest of my family.

There is a big photograph on the top of the front page of the city paper. I recognize the face of the man. I don't know him personally, but he's been a part of our mosque ever since I can remember. He's even led a youth group. I wasn't part of it, but I knew about it.

The headline is big too. Mole in Mosque Roots Out Terrorists. The peace of the prayers slips away.

"He worked with the police. He informed on his brothers!"

"He averted a disaster! He did all of us a favor!"

The opinions swirl around us. I find myself looking at their faces. Some of them I've know since I was a small boy. Could one of these not be who he seems? Could one of these be gathering information on the rest of us, reporting to police the things they hear and see that seem different or suspicious, just like Detective Moffett asked me to do? And what is suspicious, anyway?

"We are Muslims, but we are also citizens," someone says. "We have an obligation to our country to inform the police of terrorists. This man is a hero."

"He'd look more like a hero if he hadn't taken their money," Zana says. She's a fast reader, and points to something at the tail end of the article. "The police paid him. Anyone can be a hero for fifty thousand dollars."

The paper is taken back from my father and the small print at the end of the article is studied.

"Maybe he's planning to donate the money to a charity," I hear one of them say.

My father steers us toward our car.

Thirty pieces of silver, I think.

My comparative religions class is coming in handy.

CHAPTER SEVENTEEN

JAY

I SHIFTED RESTLESSLY in the pew. It was amazing how anything short of a bed of nails could be this hard and uncomfortable. Even more amazing was how much harder and more uncomfortable they became as the service went on.

The only thing other than the hardness of the pews that kept me awake was music. At least we got to stand up and sing along. There were no hymn books anymore. The words were projected onto a big screen at the front. And on the eighth day, God created technology and he saw that it was good.

The whole altar was taken up by the band. Did Jesus have a band? If he'd gone to *this* church, he would have had a backup band instead of disciples.

The drummer was pounding away at his skins. He was segregated from the rest of the band behind a clear plastic half-wall. It was supposed to be there to muffle the sound, but I think it had more to do with keeping him away from the singers. They were all female, and a couple of them were okay to look at. While they all looked pretty innocent, the drummer looked like somebody who'd been partying the night before, playing some club with a heavy metal band. He was a little rough around the edges.

I had to admit that all in all they weren't bad, and I found myself tapping my foot along with the music even if I wasn't singing. Certainly, I could sing along. All the words were right up on the big screen. And on the eighth day, God created digital projectors.

Now I knew I was getting bored.

The music stopped, the band members sat down, and the minister came to the front. He was equipped with a special hands-free microphone system that sat on his head and wrapped around his mouth. The only people I ever saw using something like that were the drive-through operators at fast food places and singers on videos. I could imagine him asking if I *wanted an apple pie with my meal*, more than I could see him belting out a tune and shaking his booty dressed in a skimpy outfit. I shuddered at that image. I needed something different in my head.

I looked up at the singers. There were at least two I *could* picture in that skimpy outfit. That was a much better visual. Thinking about that might shave a couple more minutes off the sermon. A nice little fantasy to while away the time. Maybe not the most spiritual thing to be doing, but at least I was here. Maybe God would know it was against my will, but it should still count for something.

My mother nudged me gently in the side. "Are you listening to what he's saying?" she whispered.

"Every word," I lied. Now back to my fantasy life.

"He's talking about the terrorists," she said.

My fantasy ground to a halt. I perked up my ears and sat up a little straighter.

"It's in the news and it's on the television, radio, and internet," he said. "Our little community has become known internationally as a site for terrorism. Who would have thought any of that was possible?"

Certainly not me.

"But here we sit, wondering, pondering, trying to make sense of the whole thing. How could members of this community be so filled with anger and rage that they set out a plan to kill and maim innocent people?" He paused. "Now, I know you say that they are not part of our community, our *church* community, but they are people who live on our streets, shop in our stores, work in our factories and businesses, and attend our schools.

"Why? It's a question I have asked myself, time and time again since I first became aware of this story. Why would they feel this anger? Why would they want to plan violence against people? Why would they want to take the lives of innocents? Why indeed." He paused again for dramatic effect.

"The answer, my friends, is simple. Evil. Hatred.

The Devil. They were the reasons that these people did what they did, planned what they planned. Why else would they turn against their faith—the loving, peaceful teachings of Mohammad and the Koran—and seek to kill?

"What is the answer to such hatred? Do we match anger with anger, hatred with hatred, violence with violence? An eye for an eye, a tooth for a tooth. These are the words of Exodus. So strongly is this concept believed that it is repeated time and again, in Leviticus and in Deuteronomy. These passages talk about retributive justice. They talk about vengeance against those that have been wronged. They talk about our right to seek retribution.

"While punishment is deemed proper and right, however, these passages refer to the *limits* of that punishment. A man who has been blinded in one eye has no right to blind both eyes of the person who has committed the original crime. These passages speak of limits and tolerance.

"One of my heroes is Gandhi. He said, succinctly, that an eye for an eye would make the whole world blind. And we know another man, living long before the time of Gandhi who would agree with that. His name was Jesus of Nazareth. This is what Jesus said in urging his followers. 'If anyone strikes you on the right cheek, turn to him the other also.'

"Jesus knew that the answer to hate was not hate,

but love. The answer to violence is not violence, but peace. The answer to evil is not evil, but good.

"One of the foundations of our faith, one of the principles on which we rest is simple: Love thy neighbor. Not love *some* of thy neighbors. Not love the ones who are nice or near. Certainly not love just those who are Christian. Love *all* thy neighbors.

"Our role, our duty as told to us by Jesus, is as simple as that. Show love, acceptance, tolerance, caring to all the people. As we go forth today in Jesus' name, go forth and practice what Jesus has taught. Love thy neighbors. All of them. Do as Jesus would do."

The minister sat down and the band started playing again. As people started to get up, I stayed seated. Powerful words. I wasn't used to hearing powerful words come out of this place. Certainly not words that had meaning for me.

"Are you asleep?" my father asked. He was standing over me.

"No, just thinking. Thinking about what he said."

My father looked surprised, but happy. "It's good when the sermon can do that. This one hit particularly close to home, didn't it?"

"Not so much close to home as close to school."

"My father, your grandfather, used to say that the purpose of church was to comfort the troubled and trouble the comfortable."

"I'm not sure which of those categories I fit into," I said.

"Could be both. Come on."

We waded through the crowd still lingering in the aisles. My father shook hands with some people along the way and exchanged small talk. Mom was already in the lobby talking to a woman I didn't recognize. She introduced the woman to me and my father. I shook hands and mumbled hello.

"Mrs. McMullian told me that she saw you on television," my mother said.

"Yes. I was very impressed at your efforts," she said. "Your parents must be very proud of the way you volunteered to help."

"Yes, very proud," my father said and my mother nodded in agreement.

I felt like telling everybody who asked that I wasn't really as much a volunteer as I was *ordered* to volunteer. But I didn't say anything. It felt good to have people think nice things about me. And, if it happened again, I think I really would volunteer to help.

"We've raised him to try to do the right thing," my mother said. "Sort of like today's sermon."

"That was a wonderful sermon!" the woman gushed.

"Well, we better get going. My stomach says it's getting pretty close to breakfast time," my father said. "You hungry, Jay?"

"When am I ever not hungry?"

"Good question."

It was one of the rituals of church that we always went out to Harvey's for breakfast after the service. This was the trade-off. If I came, I got bacon and eggs and pancakes. I liked bacon and eggs and pancakes. Sure, I could have the same thing if we went home, but it really wasn't the same.

— ✳ —

My mother went up to the counter and ordered while my dad and I grabbed a paper and sat down at the table. My mother always went up and got the food for us. She insisted. It was sort of like her doing the cooking. I didn't care who cooked as long as I got to do the eating.

"Front page again," Dad said. He pointed at another article about the arrests. The header over this one was Homegrown Terrorism. I was more interested in the homegrown sports section. I rummaged through the paper until I found it.

My dad made a snorting sound. "It says here that the lawyers for the accused are upset because the prisoners are being segregated and aren't allowed to meet each other. Meeting each other is what got them into trouble in the first place!"

"I guess so."

"And do you know what's really annoying to

me?" he asked. "These people have nothing but scorn for Western ways, for democracy, for freedom, but the minute they get caught they scream and holler about their rights. If they were in a Muslim country and conspired to blow up buildings, do you think they'd have any rights except the one to have a bullet put through their heads?"

I didn't think he actually wanted me to answer that question, but I was going to anyway.

"But we're not a Muslim country. Here they're supposed to be innocent until proven guilty."

"And do you think they're innocent?" my dad asked.

"I don't know anything except what I read, and that isn't much," I said.

"If the police didn't have evidence, they wouldn't have arrested them."

"And I guess we'll find out what that evidence is when it goes to court. It's just hard to believe that Azeem would be a terrorist."

"Azeem. That's the kid from your school, right? You know him?"

"He wasn't in my year, so I wouldn't say I knew him. He pretty much stayed to himself."

My father nodded. "Lots of killers are loners."

"I didn't say that. He had friends. It's just that they were brown kids, like him. The brown kids don't talk to me much."

"That sounds like racism to me," he said.

"Maybe, but I don't talk to them much either."

My mother set down the trays in front of us on the table. The food put an end to this discussion. That suited me just fine. I was just happy to have bacon for breakfast.

CHAPTER EIGHTEEN

JAY

WITH MY RIGHT PAW, I pushed up the velour sleeve of my left arm to look at my watch. It was 8:20. I'd been waiting ten minutes, and I had ten more minutes until Kevin and Steve arrived. It was amazing how slow time could pass sometimes. Especially when you were standing outside the back door of the school, wearing a bear costume and waiting for the other two bears to arrive.

I should have let Kevin pick me up and drive me to school, but my mother had said she'd drive me. Of course then she had to leave early. If only I'd been smart and let Kevin drive me. Then again, the being smart ship sailed the minute I agreed to dress up as one of the Three Bears for the Halloween assembly. So here I stood in a brown velour suit, a little tail pinned to my butt, whiskers painted on my cheeks, my nose painted black, and a little hat with ears on my head. This would have been a really cute costume—if I were five years old. And a girl.

The Three Bears wasn't our first choice. Originally we were going to go with the Three Musketeers, until we found out we couldn't have swords—even plastic swords—because that violated the board policy about "weapons or replicas." Without the swords, we would have just been three guys wearing poofy pants and frilly shirts.

A second suggestion had been the Three Little Pigs, but after the whole thing with the ham spread around Brown Town, I thought that wasn't such a good idea. Kevin thought it was a *great* idea *because* of the vandalism. He called it a "hook." The only thing I knew about hooks was that I didn't want to be strung up on one. After a lot of discussion, I was able to convince Steve that it wasn't the right thing to do or wear.

Kevin wasn't pleased when I did that. Kevin was never pleased when people didn't do exactly what he said.

"Quite the costume."

"Thanks," I mumbled without looking over. People had been making comments as they passed since I'd arrived, and it was starting to get old before the day had even started.

"What are you, like, a dog?"

"It's a bear, I'm a—" I stopped mid-sentence. I was talking to a girl—I guess it was a girl; the voice was a girl's—wearing a big black *burka* sort of outfit. Only her eyes were visible. I'd been staring out at the parking lot so intently that I hadn't seen her come up. I had to fight the urge to take a half step back. These people always unnerved me.

"I guess it could be a bear," she said.

"It is."

"Did you make it yourself?" she asked.

"No, of course not!"

"Too bad. It would have changed my whole image of the football team."

That voice sounded so familiar, but I'd never talked to one of these people before. They always just drifted down the halls, usually two or three together, whispering to themselves. It was eerie to watch them because you couldn't see their feet move. It looked as if they were being blown around like a bunch of dark rain clouds.

"I wanted to thank you for helping to clean up the vandalism," she said.

"Thanks. Did you see it on television?"

"Yes. You looked very guilty."

"Guilty? I didn't do anything wrong!"

"Now you *sound* guilty."

"I'm not guilty of anything! We weren't even here when it happened! We were at a—"

"At a football game. I know. Maybe guilty is the wrong word. Embarrassed. You looked embarrassed on television."

"Uncomfortable is more like it," I said. "Being on television wasn't my idea."

"You don't even like being in front of a class to make a presentation," she said.

Classroom... She had been in one of my classes— that's why I knew the voice. She didn't have any sort of accent, nothing foreign or strange. She sounded sort of like me, except she spoke faster.

"You're lucky that sometimes you have a really, really good partner to carry you in those presentations."

Presentation...partner...

"Zana?"

"Big football star can't remember the little people along the way," she chided.

"No, it's just that I didn't recog—" I stopped myself.

"I'm doing my hair differently."

"Yeah...right... That's it."

She laughed. "Don't be stupid. Of course you couldn't recognize me, but didn't you recognize my voice?"

"It sounded familiar, but..."

"You can see my eyes, though."

I looked down. She was a good four inches shorter than me. There, looking back at me from the shadows, were two beautiful gray-blue eyes. I always thought she had the most incredible eyes. Afghani eyes.

"Where'd you get the costume?" I asked, before I even thought not to ask.

"It's not a costume!" she snapped. She suddenly sounded angry and I knew I'd said something wrong. "This is just part of Muslim tradition."

"Your parents are making you do this?"

"My parents are *opposed* to me doing this."

I tried to figure out what to say next, but she spoke instead.

"They don't understand why I'm doing it. Neither does my brother, you know, Haroon."

"Haroon… He's in my geography class. He's your brother?"

She nodded.

"I didn't know you had a brother."

"He's my twin, and no cracks about how we don't look like twins. I think this is very confusing to him. I'm just trying to get in touch with my religion. Live my life as a devout Muslim. Life needs purpose."

I was trying to think of something deep to say in response, but I was saved from the struggle by the appearance of Kevin and Steve. Zana saw them as well, watching as they walked toward us. Two bears.

"Wow. Do I look that goofy?" I asked.

"Pretty well, but some people can pull it off," she said.

"You think I pull it off?"

"No, I said *some* people. I didn't say you were one of those people."

She laughed and I laughed along with her.

"Hey, Boo Boo. Have you seen any picnic baskets?" Steve yelled as they came loping toward me. He looked like he was enjoying this. But then again, he seemed to enjoy most everything.

"You're looking good, bro!" Steve called out as we tapped hands in greeting.

"And who's your *friend*?" Kevin asked.

"This is Zana."

"Nice costume," he said sarcastically.

"This coming from a guy dressed in a bear outfit."

"It's Halloween. I have an excuse. What's yours—bad hair day?"

"Better than having a bad brain year!" she snapped. She was quick.

Steve started to chuckle and Kevin shot him a look that shut him up.

"Big talk from somebody who doesn't have the brains to be an individual but has to dress like a big, black sheep and follow the herd," Kevin said.

"Again, this from a guy dressed identically to his two buddies. Some imagination."

"If *you* had any imagination, you'd realize that we're all dressed the same because we're the Three Bears," Kevin said.

"Like Poppa Bear, Momma Bear, and Baby Bear?" she asked.

"Exactly."

"So if Jay is the baby bear, which of you is the momma?"

"Neither of us!" Kevin said. "We're both poppa bears."

"I see. So this is sort of the gay version of that classic fairy tale. Baby Bear has *two* daddies."

This time I was the one who had to work hard not to laugh.

"It would be a touching story about two daddy bears frolicking through the forest, skipping, holding hands, picking flowers, and—"

"Why don't you shut up, you stupid sand monkey!" Kevin snarled.

My mouth dropped open. The anger in his voice, the look of hatred in his eyes startled me. Steve looked just as shocked. Kevin stepped forward and bumped into Zana. She stumbled, almost tripping as she stepped backward off the sidewalk. I grabbed him by the arm and he struggled to get free.

Steve stepped in as well, positioning himself directly between Kevin and Zana.

"It's not worth it," Steve said. "Just forget it."

Kevin didn't respond right away, but then he seemed to relax. He nodded his head and I released his arm.

"Go inside," I said. "I'll meet you two in a minute."

Steve led Kevin toward the door. He was muttering under his breath, but he kept walking. He paused at the door and looked back.

If looks could kill, she was dead.

"You okay?" I asked.

"I'm fine." She didn't sound fine. "Your friend is a bully and a jerk."

"You pushed him into a corner."

"He was the only one who did any pushing, but maybe it's good that he was pushed into a corner. Maybe then he'll understand what it's like when racists push *us* into corners."

"He's not a racist."

"Are you defending what he said?" she demanded.

"I'm not defending anything. I just know he isn't a racist."

"Then I guess he made that sand-monkey comment in an affectionate, nickname sort of way. But what else can I expect from another white but racism?"

"Are...are you calling me a racist?" I stammered, not able to believe what she was saying.

"If the sheet fits."

I shook my head. "Let me see if I understand. *All* whites are racists, is that right?"

"You got it."

"But you saying *that* isn't a racist comment, putting all of us in the same category because of our color?"

She didn't answer right away. Maybe I'd scored a point.

"Can I ask you a question?" she asked.

"Sure."

"You helped clean up the vandalism. If your friends had been the ones who had done it, would you—?"

"My friends didn't do it!" I protested. "They were with me at a football game. There were hundreds of witnesses!"

"Yeah, I know. What I'm saying is, *if* they had done it, and *if* you knew they had done it, would you turn them in?"

"Turn in my friends?"

"Yes."

I didn't know what to say. I knew the right answer, but I didn't know if that was my honest answer. Turning them in would be the right thing to do, but what sort of person would turn in his friends, be a stoolie?

"That's what I thought," she said. "There are two types of racists. Those who write and say the words and those who don't do anything about it. At least the first type is honest."

She turned on her heels and left, leaving me standing there, open-mouthed, unable to even think of what to say. I wanted to yell after her, but I wasn't sure what to yell. A couple of words came to mind and they weren't pretty. Here I'd been defending her, and now *I* was a racist? What had I done to deserve any of this?

Steve and Kevin were waiting for me just inside the door. Both were laughing and joking around. It was as if nothing had just happened.

"We are a lock for the best costume award," Steve said excitedly. "Nobody can touch us."

"How exactly does the contest work?" I asked.

"Same as last year," Steve said.

"I wasn't here last Halloween," I said.

"That's right. Let me explain it to you. We all go on the stage in the cafeteria and the audience applauds for its favorite," Kevin explained.

"How many entries do you think there'll be?"

"Last year there were over thirty," Steve said.

"More than *forty*," Kevin said, correcting him.

"Whatever. A whole lot. But quantity doesn't matter. It is a question of quality, and I haven't seen anybody who can match our quality," Steve said. "Have you?"

I'd spent most of my time standing in front of the school trying not to be seen, so I really hadn't had much of a chance to see anybody, but—

"What about him?" I asked pointing down the corridor. They both turned around.

"Jules!" Steve shouted and the guy came toward us with a big smile on his face.

I recognized him as the guy who'd been at court with Haroon. His name was Julian. He was wearing a tuxedo and in his arms was a ventriloquist's dummy, dressed like a penguin.

Steve and Julian gave each other a big hug. Kevin said hello, but it was a pretty restrained greeting. Then it all clicked. This was the guy who had been on the team last year—all-conference running back. But he had decided not to come out for the team this year. Kevin would have taken that personally.

"Nice get-up," Steve offered.

"Thank you, thank you," he said and gave a little bow. "And my compliments to the Three Bears. All you need is some blonde babe to play Goldilocks."

"Goldilocks!" Steve screamed. "That would have been perfect! Why didn't we think of that?"

"It's not too late," Julian offered. "There has to be at least one hot blonde who has a crush on a member of the football team—unless I'm remembering wrong."

"Nope. No problem there," Steve said. "I've got girls lined up at my door."

"Lined up? What, are they trying to get out?" Julian asked.

"Funny. You miss not playing?"

"I don't miss the practices."

"But you do miss the games. Admit it," Steve said.

Julian smiled. He had a big, friendly, easy-going smile. "I miss the games."

"You should have come out," Kevin said. "You would have made it a better team."

"How much better do you need to be?" Julian asked. "You're the best team in the conference with or without me."

"You got *that* right," Kevin said.

"I know," Julian said. "I've been exploring other options."

"So, what's up with the dummy?" Kevin asked.

"I don't know. What's up, Steve?"

Steve gave him a fake punch to the stomach and then a little push.

"Hey, watch the dummy, dummy! Gotta run. See you bears on the stage. Good luck!" He walked away down the hall.

"Looks like we have a little bit of competition," Steve said.

"Maybe. You won't see any member of the football team cheering for him," Kevin said.

CHAPTER NINETEEN

HAROON

THERE'S A VAMPIRE in my classroom.

And a pirate. And a devil, complete with red cape and horns.

When I was a little kid, my parents let Zana and me dress up in costumes and go trick-or-treating. "It's not part of our culture or religion," they said, "but Halloween isn't really a religious event anyway." They didn't mind making us stand out from our classmates for the big things, but they didn't consider Halloween a big thing.

But I've never been tempted to wear a costume to high school.

Still, it brightens the day and helps chase away those post-*Eid* blues to see kids in costume sitting in Ms. Singh's class, waiting for a lesson in comparative religions.

I take my seat in the desk-ring Ms. Singh has arranged and dig through my backpack for the slim binder that holds my religion notes. We don't use a textbook in this class. Ms. Singh likes to go right to the source—the Koran, the Talmud, the Bible, the

Bagadavita, the Malleus Malefactorum, the letter Luther nailed to the door.

It's the first class of the day, and kids are still trickling in, distracted and still waking up. There are clusters of kids all around the room. Some are talking about dates, some making plans. Some are gathered around a portable DVD player. There's too much chatter in the room for me to be able to decipher which movie they're watching.

"Good luck tonight," Juanita says from across the ring.

"Good luck with what?" Sonder asks. "Trick-or-treating?"

"It's the first *Reach for the Top* game," I say.

"Oh. Too bad it's tonight. We're having an all-ages drag party at the Community Center."

"I already know about it," I say. "Julian's going as a nun, and Reverend Bob is going as Sister Bob."

"Maybe you can drop by if you get back in time," Sonder says. "You'll have to dress in drag, though."

"He could dress up as his sister," one of the guys says.

I rise out of my seat. What am I going to do—hit him? Luckily, Ms. Singh breezes into the room and I don't have to do anything.

"Good morning, everyone," she says, all good cheer and energy. "Tonight is All Hallow's Eve, and I see some of you are already prepared—

unless you're running out of clean laundry."

She banters on, asking random kids questions about the origins of Halloween and theories of the devil, as everyone takes their seats and gets ready for the class.

"Movie time is over, boys. Put your toy away," she says to the students around the DVD player. Among them is Hadi. They either ignore her or are too engrossed in what they're watching. They don't look up as she walks over to them, picks up the DVD player, and turns it around to see what is on it.

For a full minute, she watches in silence. Hadi says, "Hey!" but she shuts him up with a movement of her hand.

"Sarah," she says to the girl nearest the door, "go to the AV room and borrow a television and a DVD player."

"That is not for you to see!" Hadi yells.

"It is now," Ms. Singh says. "You brought it into my classroom, and that makes it mine."

The AV room is nearby. Sarah is soon back, wheeling in the TV on a metal cart. Ms. Singh has it all plugged in and ready to go within minutes.

"I was going to regale you this morning with my rendition of Sufi love songs," she says, attempting to be funny, but there is no humor in her face or in her voice. She is trying very hard to hold herself together. "But I think, if you all don't mind postponing the songs of Rumi, that this will make a better lesson."

The classroom lights go off, the TV goes on, and into our suburban classroom comes the face of Osama bin Laden.

There is a voiceover in English. "All believing Muslims should join in *jihad* against the Jews and Americans. Death to nonbelievers! Only in this way is Allah to be praised."

It goes on like that for five minutes before Ms. Singh shuts it off. The beautiful words of the Holy Koran come out as curses. I feel sick to my stomach. The voice kept urging Muslims to kill, then hide, then kill again. The television showed things exploding, people crying, and young men with balaclavas running obstacle courses in a desert, rifles held up high and proud. Names of martyrs, and the deeds they did to get to paradise, roll past my eyes. I think of Azeem—so calm, so quiet, so good at math—and it doesn't fit.

The screen goes dark. Ms. Singh turns the lights back on. The class is silent. I don't want to look at anyone.

"Bomb them all," someone says. "The Americans should bring the neutron bomb out of storage and drop it all over the Middle East. All those crazy people will die, nothing would be damaged. We could move into their palaces and take their oil."

"That's genocide," I hear Juanita say.

"No. That's self-defense," the neutron-bomb fan says. "It's them or us. I say it's them."

"What about Indonesia?" Sonder asks. "What about India? England? Australia? There are Muslims everywhere. You figuring on killing them all?"

"And the gays along with them."

Ms. Singh likes her classroom to be a free exchange of views, where everyone can say what's on their mind. This is not the first time free speech has gotten ugly, but it's the first time it's gotten this ugly. She steps in.

"I think at this time we could *all* use some Sufi love songs." She passes out sheets of old Persian poems, and has us read and write quietly for the rest of the class. I'm relieved when the class ends.

"There are no right answers in religion," Ms. Singh reminds everyone, as we gather our books to change class. "But there are plenty of wrong ones. We need to examine religion the way we would examine a commercial on TV, or a politician's speech, to be sure we're not being sold a toxic waste dump when we think we're buying paradise."

I hang around to ask her about last-minute details for the *Reach for the Top* taping. Hadi is talking to her.

"Give me back the DVD," he orders.

"I've asked you before to talk to me with some respect, but in this case it wouldn't matter. You're not getting the DVD back. I'm giving it to the principal, and he'll likely give it to the police." She takes the DVD out of the machine and puts it in her desk drawer.

"You have no right!" Hadi says. "You are a thief. You are a criminal."

"Then I'll pay the consequences." Ms. Singh stands in front of the drawer. "If you have any more copies, I suggest you get rid of them. There's nothing there for you, Hadi. Just pain and emptiness."

Hadi's face contorts with hate and rage. I can't tell if it's from the loss of his DVD or from a woman daring to speak to him like that. I can almost see his muscles tense, and he lunges for Ms. Singh, trying to push her away from the desk. I grab him from behind, and although I can tell from the muscles in his arms that he's stronger than I am, I manage to pull him away.

"Don't be stupid," I tell him. "You could be expelled for that."

He regains control of himself, and I let him go. "You will pay!" he spits out. Then he leaves the classroom.

We both take a moment to catch our breath. "You should report him," I say. "He shouldn't get away with that."

"If I report him, then I'll have to report you too," Ms. Singh says. "Zero tolerance for fighting. You'd both be suspended. But I don't want to do it anyway. It's early in the school year. Hadi could grow a lot by June. The DVD is a police matter, though, and I will turn that in."

We discuss the final details for the show, then I hurry off to class. There's no team drill today. Ms. Singh wants us to relax, have fun, get some fresh air. I can get the air, but fun and relaxation are getting harder and harder to come by.

Chapter Twenty

JAY

"AND IT'S CLEAR that we are down to two contestants!" Mr. McCloud, the drama teacher, yelled into the microphone, his words echoing off the far wall of the cafeteria.

It was pretty obvious to me too. As he'd gone from person to person or group to group, he'd held his hand over their heads and asked the audience to cheer and applaud. For some there wasn't much more than polite applause. For others there was a good response, but nothing off the board. Then there was us and Julian. There wasn't much doubt that we were the top two choices, but I couldn't tell who was number one.

"I'd like to ask the Three Bears and Julian and Julian Junior to remain on the stage!" he announced.

There was a little bit of grumbling, but most people were okay about things. What was the point of arguing?—the audience had spoken. A few of the other contestants wished us well as they headed off. Finally, it was only the five of us left on stage—well, really six if you counted the dummy.

"The winner of this year's contest will receive the following prizes. One, a lovely autographed picture of our principal." He held it up in his hand and there was a smattering of laughter and booing. "Suitable for framing or placing on a dart board—not that I would suggest that. Two, a twenty-five-dollar gift certificate from our cafeteria. And last, but not least, Central Secondary School t-shirts! What a truly amazing gift package valued at well over twenty-five dollars. Now, this one is for all the marbles," Mr. McCloud said. "Your applause will determine the winner. First, let's hear your applause for the Three Bears!"

There was cheering and whistling and stomping. Steve pranced and posed a little. I tried not to look at anybody. This was really kind of embarrassing—but okay in a really stupid sort of way. Finally, the applause died down.

"Thank you. And now, for Julian and Junior!"

Again, there was a surge of cheering and screaming and stomping. I looked over at Steve. His expression matched my thoughts. It was louder...I thought. It went on for a good twenty seconds. Was that longer than our ovation?

Kevin was staring straight out into the audience. His expression was stone serious. Did he think they got a bigger cheer? Having to stand up in front of everybody and be declared the loser wasn't what I signed up for.

"This is close," Mr. McCloud said. "Both groups deserve to win, but it seems like the audience has spoken. The winner of this year's contest is Julian and Julian Junior!"

There was a big cheer and a bunch of people jumped to their feet. Julian rushed forward to take the picture, t-shirt, and gift certificate from Mr. McCloud. We shuffled over to the side and exited the stage, taking shelter behind the curtains. Well, at least we didn't have to stand on stage anymore. I was just happy to have the whole thing over. I hoped it meant that I didn't have to wear the bear costume for the rest of the day.

Julian grabbed the microphone. "I'd like to thank all the people who made this possible," Julian said. Well, technically, it was Julian talking but the dummy was the only one moving its lips.

"I want to thank all you voters—my fans, the little people who stood behind me all the way."

There was a cheer from the audience.

"If you want to thank me, use your gift certificate to pay for my lunch today!" somebody yelled up.

Julian ignored him. "And I want to thank my mother and my father, my teachers, and of course God. And I want you all to know that I will dedicate myself during my one-year term as Halloween costume champion to bring about world peace, end hunger, and find a cure for male pattern baldness. Thank you, all. I love you all!"

He bowed from the waist, then stood up and blew kisses out to the audience before he finally left the stage.

"That was a great acceptance speech," I said.

"If we couldn't win, I was just glad it was Jules," Steve said.

"We *could* have won," Kevin said.

"It was close."

"Did you notice who was cheering for him?" Kevin demanded.

It looked to me like a whole chunk of the school, but I figured that was not the answer he was looking for.

"Every brown face in the crowd was cheering for him. Every *last* one of them. Did you see how many cheered for us?"

I hadn't really been noticing much of anything. My focus had been on my feet.

"None. Not one," Kevin said, spitting out the words.

"Come on, Kevin," Steve said. "Some were."

"None that I saw. And do you know why?" he demanded. "Because we're white! I know you're black," Kevin added. "Well, half black. But look at the two of us. You can't get any whiter than Jay!"

"Maybe they just liked Julian's costume better," Steve said.

I did think it was a great costume. Julian might have won fair and square. But maybe Kevin had a point. We *were* pretty white. If Zana wasn't the only person who felt that way about whites, then maybe he wasn't as far off the mark as Steve thought.

"I don't think so," Kevin maintained. "They weren't voting for us no matter what. I'm tired of these people. I'm tired of the way they dress, the way they smell, the way they think they're better than us, the way they aren't grateful to live in the best country in the world. I'm just plain tired of them, and I'm tired of having to act like I should apologize for it!"

Nobody spoke. We just stood there, slightly off-stage. I think even Kevin was surprised at what he'd just said.

"Look," Steve said, "let's just get out of here for a while. Let's blow off fourth period and go for a coffee. My treat. What do you think?"

"That sounds like a good idea," I said. "Kevin?"

"Sure. Let's go."

He grabbed the hat off his head and threw the bear ears into the garbage can. I guess that answered my question about staying in costume.

— ✳ —

"I'm just tired of those people," Kevin snapped.

I thought that getting him away from the school might have helped, but he was still pretty wired. Of course, the coffee and donuts weren't the best sedatives.

"They don't come to the football games to cheer for us."

"Some come," Steve said.

"Hardly any. They're always complaining about something. It makes me sick to the stomach—all that screaming about prejudice. They bring it on themselves by walking around ignoring people, jabbering to each other in that monkey talk, keeping to themselves, thinking they're better than everybody else."

While he continued to rant, I tried to look casual as I surveyed the donut shop. It was midday, and other than the staff behind the counter—who were too far away to hear us—we had the place pretty much to ourselves.

"Forget it," Steve said. "It doesn't matter. This whole contest doesn't matter. *They* don't matter. In the end, who do you think rule the school?"

Kevin stopped talking and smiled. "We do."

"Nothing's changed. It wasn't like one of them won either. Julian had a good gimmick going on. And, if you think about it, up until this year he *was* a member of the football team."

I didn't know if that would make Kevin feel better or worse.

"You're right," he said.

Better. It had made him feel better.

"Nothing has changed," Steve said.

"You're right," Kevin agreed. "We still get to do

the things we want to do. Who do you think has more fun, us or the guys dressed in towels?"

"I don't know," Steve said. "Towels *can* be nice, depending on who you're taking a bath with."

We all laughed.

"You both know what tonight is, right?" Kevin asked.

"Of course. Halloween."

"Exactly. And I think it's time for us to have more fun than the average bear. I'll pass the word on to the other guys. We'll meet behind the school at nine."

I couldn't help but think about Brown Town and the vandalism.

"What do you have in mind?" Steve asked.

"Not sure yet. But the school is a good place to meet. We'll go from there once we know how many guys and how many vehicles we have."

Good, we were going to leave the school.

"And remember to wear dark clothes and bring a mask. Something to hide your face. I'll bring everything else we'll need."

My sense of relief quickly evaporated.

CHAPTER TWENTY-ONE

HAROON

WE LEAVE RIGHT AFTER SCHOOL, crammed into Ms. Singh's rusty old blue Dodge Shadow. There's a rehearsal, so we can all get used to using the buzzers, then a dinner break. The show provides sandwiches, but Ms. Singh says it's too soon to get cozy with the enemy (she means the team from Rutherford High in the next county), so she takes us out for Chinese food. She keeps us laughing with tales of all the things that have gone wrong on her travels. She and her friend Ruth, an Israeli teacher who lives in Jerusalem, only get to see each other on school breaks, and they always meet up in some place like Lourdes or Busan or Ayer's Rock with their back-packs and their hitchhiking thumbs. When you travel like that, things always go wrong, although often in a good way. We laugh so much our nerves go away, and we are able to get enough protein and carbohydrates into us to keep us going through the competition.

I've never been in a television studio, and even though this is local public television, not Rockefeller Center, it's still exciting. I'm almost too excited to be nervous. People are rushing around, looking like they have important things to do and know how to do them. I've visited my mother at her work many times and seen that same look of important busyness in people who work at the hospital. The difference, of course, is that at the hospital, work is life and death. At a television studio, the stakes are not nearly as high.

As Ms. Singh says, it's only a quiz show.

They put makeup on all of us, even us guys. "You'll look like the undead if you go under those TV lights without a bit of color," the makeup artist says. She has a thick Yorkshire accent. "That may be fine for Halloween tonight, but the show won't air for another week," she adds, dabbing rouge and other stuff on my face.

"Women do this every day?" I say, marveling at the hassle.

"Oh, sure. Some ladies don't go anywhere without their makeup and masks on."

— ✳ —

I'm sitting with the rest of my team on the stage, which is called the floor, all black with tape marks to show where folks are supposed to stand. There's a great deal of worry among the technicians that we don't trip on cords. The cords are covered over, but they tell us—numerous times—to be careful anyway.

I guess they're used to dealing with adolescents who have more growth than grace.

My family is in the audience, front row. Zana is getting some looks and whispers from people in the audience. If she knows, she doesn't show it. My parents know, though. My mother puts her hand on Zana's arm, and my father leans in with a big smile to tell her a joke he's probably told her a hundred times before. The three of them laugh. I love that about my family. We fight, but we stick together.

Zana is far from the strangest-looking person in the audience. I'd say that award would have to go to the girl two rows back—hair in orange spikes and white powder on her skin, making the heavy black eye makeup and lipstick stand out. Her parents are leaning *away* from her. I have a quirky desire to get her and Zana together. They're both independent. I bet they'd like each other.

"They're dressing alike to intimidate us," Nadia says, nodding toward the Rutherford team. They're not a uniform school, but tonight they're all wearing black turtlenecks.

"They look like beatniks," Nadia says. "Somebody pass them some bongos and espresso."

My face feels funny. I start to think about all the women in the audience with makeup on their faces. But my thoughts are interrupted by a production assistant. She hands me a three-by-five card and a pen.

"Write down something interesting about your-self," she tells all of us. "When Betty introduces you, you'll want her to have something to say, right? Now's the chance to impress your friends, tell your secrets, confess your sins. One or two lines will do. Print. Legibly."

I know about this from previous shows, and Ms. Singh has reminded us to be thinking of something to write, but I'd put it out of my mind. What's inter-esting about me? I have a very smart sister, a mother who's a doctor, and a father who's a professor. *They* are interesting. The only interesting thing about me is that I'm on the *Reach for the Top* team. And I can't very well put that down.

The Rutherford team is writing, scratching out, snorting, and pushing each other. They ask for more cards. My own team is more refined. I can see they've all got something written. I lean in, thinking I can steal an idea, but then I think of something on my own. It's daring, but it feels right, and I don't hesitate.

The cards are collected and someone comes out to talk to the audience, explain the rules, and rev them up. Then we're told to take our places.

The lights are bright in my eyes. I can hardly see the audience, but I can sense they're there. Feet shuf-fle, someone coughs.

I put all other thoughts out of my mind. "Pretend

you're back in my classroom," Ms. Singh has advised us. "Rely on your brains. You've trained them well."

I take a very deep breath. I've trained. I'm ready. We all are.

The director cues, the cameras light up, the announcer booms, "It's time to play *Reach for the Top* Game One of the Regional Championships. It's Rutherford High vs. Central Secondary. Please welcome your host, Betty Olsen!"

All energy and enthusiasm, Betty bounds onto the stage. She's a younger version of Ms. Singh (although Ms. Singh doesn't need to look at the answers). Within moments, we are into the game.

"First round—snappers! For ten points each."

Questions are snapped out, and answers tossed back just as quickly.

"Elemental symbol for Polonium."

"Po."

Metric equivalent of the pennyweight."

"1.555 grams."

"Latin word for thirteen."

"Tredecim."

On it goes. Our teams are evenly matched. Rutherford makes early gains out of the gate, but then they get overconfident and start to fumble. We close the gap.

After a couple of rounds of questions, Betty stands between the two teams. "Now let's meet the teams," she says. In her hands are the three-by-five cards we filled out.

The Rutherford team goes first. Its members' "interesting points" vary from a love of mustard to a hobby of developing a database on all the kings and queens in history.

Then it's our turn. The other three go first. I'm the most recent member of the team, so I'm at the far end.

"And this is Haroon," Betty says, still beaming and energetic. She has no idea of what the words on the card she's holding are going to mean to some people. "Haroon, you have someone you'd like to say a special hello to."

"Yes," I say, plunging in quickly so I can't chicken out. "I'd like to say hello to Azeem. He was originally part of the team, but he had to drop out. I'd like to say hi and thanks for the coaching."

Betty turns to the camera and smiles. "Azeem, if you're watching, a big hello from all of us. Now, on to the theme round."

I can see Ms. Singh. She gives me a thumbs-up. I can't see my parents because of the bright lights, but I like to think they're proud that I did that. For all their worrying, they value kindness above security. Anyway, *I'm* proud of what I did.

We are halfway through the theme round—four questions on a common theme, in this case, Royal

Rascals—when the director calls a halt. "We need everyone to leave the studio immediately," she says. I see two police officers come onto the floor. "Everyone, please step outside. The staff will guide you out."

My brain is still in quiz mode. So is the host's. She goes over to the director to start to argue. The director says something quietly to her, then Betty is back with us, shooing us out, telling us to hurry and to "watch out for the cords."

We are all taken outside to a parking lot. I join my family.

"Please, everybody, stay together. I'm sure it's nothing and we'll be back inside in a moment."

"What's happening?" I hear a parent ask. "Is there a fire?" Fire trucks are already there, and another one arrives as we gather.

"A bomb threat was phoned in to the studio," the director says, trying with the tone of her voice to make it sound like it was no big deal. "Probably just a kid doing a Halloween prank. The police will check out the building, then we'll go back in and finish the show."

Just a kid, I think, and it's on the tip of my tongue to say which one. I leave my family and go over to Ms. Singh. She knows what I'm thinking before I say anything.

"There's no proof," she says.

"He threatened us," I say quietly.

"There's no proof," she says again. "Do you want to live in a country where people can be accused without proof? This is out of our hands. Keep your head in the game. Stand with your teammates. Pretend you're still in the studio."

It's silly advice, but strangely, it works. Rutherford High is bouncing around, its members scattered to family and school friends. We stand together, keeping our thoughts still. It makes a difference when we're given the all clear soon after and allowed to go back in the studio. It doesn't take long for the machinery of the show to crank back into place. I take my spot behind my buzzer, endure the makeup woman dabbing stuff on my face, and we're ready to roll.

We start with another theme round, our scores even. Rutherford is having trouble getting their concentration back. Their answers to Tall Tales questions are all over the place. Our score takes a great leap forward.

We get a moment to catch our breath when Betty gives everyone the rundown on the prizes and introduces the judges.

"Are you all right?" Nygen asks me.

"What? Of course," I say.

"You look angry."

"I am," I say. "I'm also all right."

I don't know for sure who called in the bomb threat. There are people everywhere who like to play stupid pranks—although playing one on the local public television station isn't likely to be an obvious choice. I know I can't be certain it was Hadi, but the fact that it could be is enough to make me furious.

I've had enough. From the harassment of Zana, to being thought of as an informer, to the messing up of Brown Town. I've had it with ignorance. It's one thing to be uninformed. It's another thing to choose to be stupid.

I am so angry, I ride that buzzer like a flying machine. I answer questions before they're even out of the host's mouth. I answer questions about things I don't even know I know. I rule that show. My teammates back me up, but mostly they just clear the field and let me go.

We obliterate Rutherford. We do it with our minds, and when the show is over, we shake their hands, show them respect, and let them go on their way.

Why can't all battles be like this?

CHAPTER TWENTY-TWO

JAY

I TOOK THE BOTTLE and brought it up to my lips. I tipped it back but pushed my tongue forward to stop any of the whiskey from actually entering my mouth. The little bit that leaked through tasted like iodine and burned my mouth. I wanted to spit it out or rinse out my mouth, but I couldn't. I couldn't do that for the same reason I couldn't say no thank you when it was passed my way. This was easier. Nobody would notice I wasn't drinking. To everybody else it just looked like I was being one of the guys. I *was* one of the guys.

It was a big circle of guys. There were eleven of us now—all members of the football team. These guys were my friends, the people I knew best and trusted the most. We'd gone to war together. They were like my family—no, that wasn't right. Not a family—a tribe.

Strange, I should have felt comfortable being here. But I had a bad feeling in the pit of my stomach.

We were hidden away in a corner of the parking lot at the back of the school, a little nook behind the auto shop. Kevin had assured us there wasn't even a camera aimed at this section. Nobody could see us from the street. Not us or the three cars. It was almost completely dark and we were safely enveloped by the shadow of the school. It didn't hurt that it was late—almost ten o'clock—late enough that all the little kids were finished trick-or-treating and were off the streets.

The bottle came around again. I looked at the label. Scotch Whiskey—Aged Seven Years. I guess it would take that long to make something taste that bad.

"You planning on reading or drinking?" one of the guys asked.

"Drinking." I put it up to my lips again and faked taking a snort.

I passed the bottle. James passed it to the next guy without taking a drink. James, along with Kevin and Paul, were driving and none of the drivers was drinking. I liked that. We were socially responsible before going out to cause havoc.

Everybody had a mask perched atop their head. The masks probably said something about the person who was going to be wearing it. Steve had a clown mask. Kevin was a vampire. I was wearing my favorite cartoon character and all-round amphibian superhero, Leonardo, the leader of the Teenage Mutant Ninja Turtles. Hero in a half shell—Turtle

Power. I'd had the mask since I was a kid and I'd dug it out of my old toy box.

The other masks included Freddy Kruger, a zombie, a skeleton, a mummy, a gorilla, a dog with a very happy expression, and two guys wearing the Scream get-up. It was bizarre watching the bottle get passed from person to person, the masks looking down from the top of everybody's head.

"Now, if everybody has had enough liquid courage we can begin," Kevin started.

"Where are we going?" one of the guys asked.

"If I told you it wouldn't be a surprise. Just follow me."

"Can't we have a clue?" James asked.

Kevin smiled. "I'll only tell you that our first stop has a connection to one of the schools we simply love to play. Let's saddle up!"

There were a lot of hoots and hollers as we climbed into the cars. I jumped into the back seat of Kevin's car, Steve up front. One of our linemen, Junior, climbed in beside me. Of course, I didn't know what was going to happen, but I was pretty happy to be part of it.

Kevin squealed out of the parking lot, laying rubber. I looked behind us as James's car and a van followed behind him. Kevin pushed in a CD and AC/DC came to life!

What could be better Halloween music than

"Highway to Hell?" Steve reached over and turned the music up full blast, so the speakers behind my head felt like they were *in* my head.

> *My friends are gonna be there too*
> *I'm on the highway to hell*
> *On the highway to hell*
> *Highway to hell*
> *I'm on the highway to hell!*

Steve started singing along and then the rest of us joined in. We got louder and louder, singing along, out of key but safely concealed by the music and the masks.

> *No stop sign*
> *Speed limits*
> *Nobody's gonna slow me down*

— ✳ —

Kevin flicked off the lights, turned off the music, and slowed the car down. I didn't even want to breathe. He pulled the car over to the side of the road, and the other two vehicles pulled in behind us. It was a quiet residential street with trees so big and full that the streetlights were lost amongst the branches and the street was dark. There were houses on one side of the street. Nice big houses set back from the street, protected by long driveways, lawns, and flowers. On the other side were trees. A park. A small forest in the middle of the subdivision.

We climbed out of the vehicles. Everybody instinctively knew to be quiet, even trying to close the doors without making too much noise. Kevin went to the back of his car and opened the trunk. The interior light in the trunk shone brightly so we could see the contents.

I couldn't believe my eyes. Inside were heads of lettuce and tomatoes, and dozens of rolls of toilet paper and flats of eggs. There was a collective gasp. People were amazed and impressed by the supplies— by the ammunition.

"Help yourselves. But remember, this is just one stop of many."

"How many?" somebody asked.

"I'm thinking four, but you never know."

Greedily people reached in and grabbed, filling their pockets and hands. I didn't want any eggs in my pockets but I grabbed a couple of tomatoes, three eggs, and a roll of toilet paper.

I looked across the street at the houses. One of them had a few lights on, a second was pitch black, and a third had every light in the whole house blazing. I was hoping for the one in the middle. Maybe nobody was home or, if they were, they were all asleep. The street itself was quiet and deserted.

"Follow me," Kevin said.

To my surprise, he didn't head across the street but into the forest. We all followed behind. It was instantly darker than on the street. We stepped into the shadows and basically vanished. We headed along a dark, narrow trail, a bumpy dirt path that weaved between the trees and bushes. The guy in front of me stumbled over a root and cursed loudly. He was instantly shushed into silence.

The trees gave way to grass. We crossed through the outfield of a deserted baseball diamond. We slipped out the other side of the field and then came to stop behind some bushes edging another street. There was a lot of huffing and puffing, mainly from the linemen. You would have figured by now they'd be in better shape.

"We're here," Kevin said as the last of the stragglers joined us.

"Yeah," one of them puffed. "But why didn't we just *drive* here? We got cars."

"Cars have license plates. Cars can be traced. By putting the cars on the other side of the park, we can't be connected to anything that is going to happen."

That was smart. That was Kevin. It was like he was calling a play in the huddle.

"So, what are we going to do?" Steve asked. "Or, I guess, to *whom* are we going to do it?"

"See that house right there?" Kevin said. "The one with the really nice flowers and that clean white Mustang in the driveway?"

"I know that car," somebody said.

"Maybe you do. It belongs to the coach of the Streetsville Stingers football team."

"Which one? Which coach?"

"The big one, the head jerk, the head coach—the one who called us bad sports."

"How do you know that he lives here?" James asked.

"Easy. I followed him home from his school last week."

"You did what?"

"Followed him. A little planning for tonight. I was sort of the advance scout."

I looked past the car to the house. There was a light on the porch and a light in an upstairs window, but the rest of the house was dark. He was probably upstairs in his bedroom but not asleep yet.

"Everybody put their hands in," Steve said. "Remember we're all in this together. If anybody gets caught you take the fall, but you don't rat out anybody else. Agreed?"

Everybody agreed. A couple of the guys were too loud and they were quieted down.

"We go in fast, we get out fast, we get to the cars, and we get outta here. Everybody put on your masks."

We all pulled them on. We were one freaky-looking group.

"Okay, break."

This was all so familiar, and safe, and foolproof. Just like football—Kevin calling the play and us following through. He told us what to do and we did it. We all fanned out, trying to move silently as we crossed the street and moved toward the house.

"Get the tires first," Kevin hissed. "Flatten the tires."

Four people, one on each wheel, bent down. In the silence, I could hear the air escaping as they pressed down on the valves. The tires flattened and the car lowered.

"Now!" Kevin yelled.

A hailstorm of eggs, tomatoes, and toilet paper were thrown at the house, car, and bushes—smashing, crashing, thumping, and thudding as they hit their marks. I threw a second egg, then a tomato, then the third egg.

Suddenly another light came on downstairs and the front door flung open. It was the Streetsville coach. He was in his boxers, with a bare chest and feet, screaming.

An egg smashed against his face.

He stumbled backward with the impact and then roared with anger. He was like some large, wounded water buffalo. He was close enough that I could see the expression on his face, glaring through the egg. I felt a rush of fear and adrenaline surge through my body.

We all started running, sprinting across the grass. Only Steve was in front of me. I stole a glance backward, looking through the edges of the mask's eyeholes. Everybody else was coming, the big linemen making better time than they ever did in the wind sprints at practice. Way behind them, I saw the Streetsville coach. He was screaming and yelling and chasing, but he was old and slow and fat—and he was falling farther behind as we ran. There was no way he could catch us. He was mad but his anger only gave all of us more fear, and that produced more speed.

We hit the outskirts of the trees and Steve ripped off his mask. I did the same. Hidden in the shadows we stopped and looked back.

Scattered across the outfield, their arms and legs pumping as hard as each of them could, was an assortment of masked characters. Way back, still out on the street, the Streetsville coach stood yelling, screaming, swearing—so angry and so loud that it felt like he was a lot closer than he was.

The next two in line caught up to us and skidded to a stop. The others were closing in. Only two of the big linemen were still in the distance.

Suddenly the coach spun around and started running back toward his house then jumped into his car. He must have figured we were cutting through the park to our vehicles on the other side.

He squealed backward and started to drive—before coming to an abrupt halt on his four flat tires. I'd forgotten about that.

The last of the linemen came chugging up, almost collapsing into the bushes, huffing and puffing.

"I knew letting the air out of those tires would come in handy," Kevin said. "But let's hustle anyway before he gets the cops here. Come on! Let's go!"

— ✳ —

There was a certain high involved with the whole thing. Driving in the car with the music pounding and the guys yelling, sneaking up to the houses silently, barraging them with eggs and vegetables and toilet paper. Then there was the danger and, of course, the fear of getting caught. It was like being in a football game, except losing this one might involve getting caught and thrown in jail.

Definitely a different penalty than ten yards for holding.

We'd been to two more places. The first of those had been dark and stayed dark. If anybody was home, they weren't even going to turn on the lights. I was told who lived there. It was Mr. Perkins. He taught business at our school. I had never been in any of his classes, but I knew him to see him. I'd heard that he was a pain in the butt and was always hassling people in the hall for no good reason. And he liked failing people. He almost caused a couple of the guys to become disqualified for football because he was such a hard marker. Other teachers gave football players a break, which was only fair because we were working so hard to represent the school. Not him. What a jerk.

Despite it all, I couldn't help but think what it would have been like for him to be in the house when the bombardment started. It would have been pretty eerie to be sitting there in the dark while your house was assaulted. He wouldn't know who it was exactly, but he had to know it was students from his school. I wondered if his wife was with him or if he had kids or whatever. I didn't like him, but I could picture his face. I tried to block out that picture. I forced myself *not* to picture him, *not* to imagine his family.

The last house had been dark, but when we got closer, a motion detector kicked in and lit up the whole front yard. We stood there, wearing our masks, arms back, eggs in hand ready to throw.

Everybody froze, exposed by the light.

Then Kevin yelled and threw the first egg. We all snapped into action. It was even stranger watching the explosion of the eggs, the flight of the tomatoes, the way the light reflected off the brilliant white rolls of toilet paper as they hit the trees, house, and hydro wires.

In spite of the light, maybe *because* of the light, the

people inside didn't even poke their heads out. They could see how many of us there were. The Streetsville coach had been brave, or stupid—or just so angry that he didn't think when he ran out after us. I wondered what I would have done if it was my house. At least I'd never have to picture the people inside the last house. It was a former principal of the school—gone before I got there.

— ✳ —

The car slowed down and we turned into the parking lot of a small park. There was a darkened tennis court on one side, a deserted playground on the other, and a large stretch of grass reached out into the distance. This looked familiar. With all the driving in the dark, blurred by the music and excitement, I'd lost any sense of where we were. But we were back in our general area...at least I thought we were.

We got out of the vehicles and gathered around the jungle gym. Nobody was even trying to be quiet anymore. Somebody pulled out a bottle and passed it around. This time I took a bigger sip. It still tasted like poison, but it was part of the experience. It burned a track down my throat and into my stomach.

People were joking, laughing, pushing. There was a real sense of excitement, of being part of something. Just like a football game and this was halftime. Replace the masks with helmets, the dark clothes with uniforms, and the smell of whiskey with sweat. I was feeling the high of the game.

"This is our last stop of the night," Kevin said.

"Come on, let's keep going!" somebody yelled and others called out in agreement.

I was one of them. That surprised me. I had been so reluctant to get started, so scared after that first house, and now I wanted things to keep going. There was a high to this. It made me feel like I was a part of something. We were in this together.

"We're running out of ammunition, and it's getting late," Kevin said. "And we do have a practice tomorrow at 7:30."

There was a collective groan. Practice, football.

"How about if we don't do any wind sprints 'cause we did them tonight?" James asked and the groans were replaced by laughs.

"Sure. You explain why to Coach Pruit," Kevin said. "Let's just finish it up right. This is like the fourth quarter. No easing up."

We hurried to the back of his car.

"I want it cleaned right out," Kevin said.

People reached in grabbing the last of the eggs, tomatoes, and toilet paper until there was nothing left. Kevin reached in, grabbed the empty egg flats, and threw them on the ground.

"There. No evidence left in the car." He closed the trunk with a thud.

We left the cars behind and started across the park. It was so dark that the few scattered street-lights couldn't penetrate into the park at all. We picked up speed as we traveled. The adrenaline was kicking in again.

"Just follow my lead," Kevin said.

We came out of the park and as one, we pulled down our masks. We ran down the street and cut onto a second, staying right in the middle of the street, like we owned it. If a car was to come along, I don't know if we would have hidden or forced it to get out of our way. We had a sense of power, of purpose.

The houses were all dark. It was almost midnight and everybody was probably tucked in bed for the night.

"Here's the place," Kevin said.

It looked identical to all the other houses on the street—a bungalow, set back from the street. Big lawn, flowers in front. If they had a car, it was in the garage.

"Everybody wait," Kevin said.

We stopped and Kevin crept up toward the house by himself. There were no motion detectors to trigger and the house remained dark. Kevin stopped by the garage. He pulled something out of his pocket... something metal...I could see the light reflect off it. He held it up, and then I heard a hissing sound and instantly knew what he was doing. He was spray-painting something on the side of the garage.

I suddenly pictured Kevin spraying words on the side of the school and on the benches of Brown Town...

But of course he couldn't have done that. He was with us at the football game.

He finished and motioned for us to come forward. Slowly we closed in on the house, fanning out across the whole front.

"Now!" Kevin yelled as he threw the first egg.

Instantly every arm flung something at the house, and the throws were accompanied by yells and shrieks. Eggs, tomatoes, and toilet paper littered the house and property.

Within thirty seconds, everybody had tossed everything they had, but there was no response from the house. It remained dark. But instead of just running away, one of the guys ran up to the porch, grabbed a flowerpot, and threw it against the house. It smashed against the wall into a million pieces. Other guys rushed forward, grabbed the rest of the pots out front, and threw them against the sidewalk and porch and house.

Kevin grabbed a flowerpot and lifted it over his head. He threw it and there was a tremendous crash as it smashed through the front picture window.

Everybody froze, shocked.

Lights came on in the neighboring house, and then a second house three doors down lit up. All at once, we all started running back down the street, heading for the park.

I was well in front of the pack and I looked back over my shoulder. The house was still dark. Maybe nobody had been home. Maybe they had been home and were huddled together—hiding, afraid. I just hoped nobody was standing at that window when it shattered.

We ran across the park. That smashed window had given everybody an extra jolt of energy. Quickly we got into the cars and sped away—Kevin leading, the other two vehicles following.

He hadn't put on the music again. The only sound was the panting of our breath. Nobody was talking. I couldn't get out of my mind the picture of that pot smashing through the window. It was loud and spectacular. And dangerous. The eggs and tomatoes were one thing, but we had crossed the line. If there had been another pot right there beside me, I might have thrown it too. And that scared me most of all.

Safely away from the area, Kevin slowed down and turned off the road and into a mall. It was late and all the stores were closed, the lights off behind big glass windows. He pulled around the side of the last store to the back. The other two cars followed.

We were now shielded on one side by the stores and on the other three by a large cement barrier fence. He came to a stop and turned off the engine. As the other two cars stopped and turned off their lights, it became dark. We all climbed out and gathered around Kevin.

"Gentlemen, that concludes our night. Everybody give me your mask."

He held out a plastic grocery bag and one by one everybody dropped their mask into it. I followed along.

"The only evidence linking us to the events of tonight is now in this bag," he said. He tied the bag in a knot and then tossed it into a dumpster behind one of the stores. "If anybody asks where you were or what you did tonight, what are you going to answer?"

"James's place, watching a movie," somebody said.

"That's right," James said. "We were all at my place. Lucky for us my father is out of town on business and my mother went with him. So we had the house to ourselves, right?"

Everybody laughed and agreed.

"What movie did we see?" Kevin asked.

"Um...*Nightmare on Elm Street*," James said. "I own the DVD."

"Everybody's seen it, right?" Kevin asked and we

all nodded in agreement. Who wouldn't have seen that movie?

"So that's what we say if anybody asks us," Kevin continued.

"But who's going to ask us?" I questioned.

"Parents, friends—whoever. It's late, and a school night."

I couldn't help but wonder about the *whoever* part.

"What happened tonight stays here," Kevin said. "We tell nobody. No friends, no girlfriends, who could become ex-girlfriends and rat us out. Not even the other members of the team. And we don't talk to each other about it for a few weeks. Agreed?"

Again, there was a chorus of agreement. I certainly wasn't going to tell anybody. That was for sure.

"Hands in," Kevin said.

One by one, we placed our hands on top of each other until we formed one big pile.

"On three… One…two…three… "

"Break!" we all yelled.

CHAPTER TWENTY-THREE

HAROON

THE VICTORY is sweet and the drive home is good.

"You sure had a fire under you in the second half," Mom says. She is driving. Dad doesn't like driving after dark. It bothers his eyes.

"The triumph of reason over fear," I say, savoring the sound of the phrase; I wonder if I'll remember it long enough to tuck it into an essay somewhere. I am relaxed for the first time in ages. We'll have to keep drilling, of course, and there will be another match in a couple of weeks. But for the moment, I am happy.

I didn't disgrace myself. I didn't let the team down. I find myself glad that Azeem had to drop out, since it gave me a chance. I almost feel bad about that, then I let it go. Azeem didn't have to leave the team because of anything I did or failed to do. There's nothing wrong about being glad when an unfortunate event has a good outcome, at least for me.

We are late getting back, late for a school night. I hope Julian is having fun at his party. He'd wanted to come to the taping, but he had to be at the party since it was a fundraiser for the local branch of a pediatric AIDS organization, and he was on the organizing committee. I briefly consider heading over there—not in the required drag, but Julian would let me in. Then as Mom turns the corner into our neighborhood, fatigue settles around me. I'll just go straight to bed. Victory or no victory, it's after midnight and there is still school in the morning.

"You had fun?" Dad asks.

"I did," I say. The whole evening had been like a dream, all that excitement and adrenaline, all those congratulations. "Maybe I'll go into broadcasting," I say.

"One local television show and you're deciding your career?" Zana asks. Zana changes her career choices almost as often as she changes her socks. Currently, it's sports medicine and recreation. Last year, it was an airline pilot.

"I think it was all that urgency without importance," I say. "Lots of crisis, but none of it is anything that can't be fixed. All the excitement of Mom's job, but without the possibility of death."

"There's a lot of excitement in being an English professor too," Dad says, only half joking. "Propping up a dangling participle, shooting stern looks at students with tardy essays, approaching the lecture podium to relate a controversial theory about Anne Hathaway. Oh, the chills!"

We all laugh and banter silly stuff back and forth,

everyone kidding everyone as we roll through the Halloween streets. We are still laughing as Mom steers the car up the driveway of our house.

The laughter stops as suddenly as if it had been cut with an axe.

Our beautiful house, beautiful because it is our home, has been savaged.

Garbage and paint, broken pots and broken windows, bushes trampled and eggs dripping everywhere. This is what greets us.

"Stay inside the car," my father says, as he opens his own door. "Whoever did this could still be around."

I see red-flashing lights as a police car pulls up in front of our house. We all get out of the car. At least the officers are not the ones who've been bothering me at school.

"One of your neighbors called it in," the officer says. "We've had a string of these tonight. Halloween. Used to be that it was enough to throw toilet paper into tree branches." He looks at Zana, keeps his face expressionless, and takes out his notebook. I leave Mom and Dad to deal with him. Zana and I join the other officer. He's shining the bright beam of his flashlight over our house to survey the damage.

It's worse in the light.

"You'll want to scrub that egg off right away," he advises. "It's nasty when it dries and hardens." The light beam swoops slowly across our home. The big picture window in the front of our house is shattered. We will be finding broken glass in our living room for months, I'm sure.

My anger rises again, but this time there's no quiz show to channel it through.

I'm sure it's the work of Hadi and his friends. *This* is *jihad*? *This* is something that would make Allah happy? I am furious with Hadi, my fists clenching and unclenching, my teeth grinding.

Zana pulls me away, into the backyard. "Calm down!" she says. "You don't want the police to see you like this. You want to be in control when they're around."

I don't even try to explain why I'm so angry. I stand in the backyard with my sister—in this lovely, private world we all created, with benches and shrubs, and one of those swings where the seats face each other, and the basketball net where Zana regularly thrashes me. We are good people! We give to charity, volunteer in the community, obey the laws, and don't bother the neighbors. We don't deserve this!

"It can all be repaired," Zana says. "It looks bad, but we'll clean it up and repair the glass. How can you be so angry about a stupid prank?"

Her words do not help. There's enough light from the neighbors' homes for me to be able to see

Zana, or what she allows me to see, in that foreign black garment. It becomes a symbol of all the craziness that's been swirling around me.

"I just want a quiet life!" I yell, and then I do something I can't believe I have it in me to do.

I rip the veil from my sister's face, and hurl it to the ground.

We stand nose to nose. I wish we were still young enough to battle it out like we used to. She may be smarter, but I'm angrier. At long last, we would be evenly matched.

"Haroon! Zana!" I hear our mother calling. "Where are you?"

"Coming," we reply automatically, in unison, in that singsong way we used to when we were kids.

I try to prolong the glare, as does Zana, but it's no good. We start to giggle. Something has been repaired. I pick up her *niqab*, shake the dirt from it, and hand it back to her. "Sorry," I say.

She accepts it but leaves it in her hand, and doesn't put it back on her face. "Do you think you know who did this?"

I tell her about Hadi, about the DVD and the outburst in Ms. Singh's classroom. "I think he called in the bomb threat, and I think he did this."

"But you have no proof," she reminds me. I tell her she sounds like Ms. Singh. It's a compliment, and she knows it.

"Zana! Haroon!" Mom calls again, but this time there's something else in her voice, something that says, *Now!*

We run out to the front yard. The police and their flashlights have found something we hadn't seen at first.

My theories about Hadi go out the window.

At the base of the house, in ugly letters, are the words Camel Jockies Go Home.

— ✳ —

Fear of Terror.

I wake up with these words on my brain. Did I hear them on TV? Did I read them in a headline?

Fear of Terror. Terror of Fear.

Fear of Fear.

I can't stop thinking about these words, and even though it's very early and none of us got to bed until very late, I get up. I put on my robe, go to my desk, turn on the lamp, and write them down.

Fear of Terror.

They look slightly ridiculous, staring up at me from a page of three-ring paper.

Isn't this what it all comes down to? All the hysteria, all the informing, all the slurs against Muslims and the bin Laden DVDs. All of it is working together in some weird way to produce the final result. People are afraid of being afraid.

243

Fear is so unpleasant that we grab on to anything that promises to relieve us of it.

Hadi takes refuge in hatred, just like the kids who messed up Brown Town and our house. They're really pretty much the same. They both strike out first so they won't feel afraid.

I doodle while I think, allowing little bits of ideas to form and dissipate, the sort of thinking I haven't indulged in much lately. Usually, it's school assignments, or prep for *Reach for the Top*. Thinking and studying with a goal in mind.

No goal this time, except understanding.

And then I think of the exceptions, of the people I know who simply refuse to play the fear game, who move through the world without being afraid of fear. Julian. Ms. Singh. My sister. So it *is* possible.

But it's not just empty fear, I remind myself. People *are* dead. There is something to fear. Mangled steel in Manhattan, a burning plane in Pennsylvania, bombs exploding without warning. This is not just an intellectual exercise. People are really dead. The War on Terror has a real purpose.

Then I add those three words underneath the first three. War on Terror. It means bombs falling from the sky, dropped by citizens from my home on top of citizens of my ancient land. All of them are just as dead.

Is the only way to fight fear to make other people

afraid? Does terrorizing others really make our own terror go away? With billions of years of evolution behind us, is this the best we human beings can come up with?

I turn off the lamp and leave my room. My father is in the living room, bundled up in a chair, making sure no one breaks into our house. A blanket is taped over the broken window. We weren't able to get anyone to come out and fix it last night. He's dozed off but jerks awake when I walk into the room.

"Go to bed," I tell him. "I'm awake now."

"No, no. You need your sleep," he mumbles.

"Let me take my turn," I say. "It's my house too. Go to bed."

He does, touching his hand to my arm as he passes by. I make myself a cup of instant hot chocolate and await the day.

— ✳ —

It's a good thing I didn't join *Reach for the Top* to become a big man on campus. An announcement of our win is made over the PA along with the other morning business. I don't hear any cheers coming from classrooms—*that* is reserved for football victories. Doesn't matter. We still won.

Then I hear Julian's voice on the PA. "I guess you are all still on some Halloween sugar high that's affected your hearing. Let me say it again, and let the outpouring of gratitude commence. *The Reach for the Top* team WON last night!"

That gets them cheering. Sure, maybe they're cheering more for the fun of making noise than because they really care that we won. But a cheer is a cheer, and I ride the wave of it with joy. Good old Julian.

CHAPTER TWENTY-FOUR

JAY

IT WAS GOOD THAT PRACTICE WAS OVER. My stomach was queasy and my legs were still burning. Last night's wind sprints hadn't really helped and the lack of sleep had definitely been a problem. It wasn't just that I had gotten in late but that I couldn't sleep when I did get to bed. It was mostly the leftover adrenaline—and there was plenty of that floating around in my system. The whole night kept playing around in my head. Parts of the night had been fun. The last part—the pot through the big glass window—had been awful. I didn't even want to think about it. When I finally did wake up, the whole thing seemed like some sort of bizarre dream.

All around me, scattered on the benches in the dressing room, were the guys who had been with me last night. Nobody talked about it. We kept our word. But nobody seemed able to make eye contact with the other members of the team. It wasn't that we were trying to avoid giving anything away. It was different. I got the feeling that nobody felt particularly proud of what had happened.

The person who showed it the most was Steve. He hadn't been himself all morning. He wouldn't joke around as usual. He wouldn't smile. A couple of times he'd jumped on people who tried to kid around—people who weren't there last night.

He sat by himself in the far corner of the room and finished dressing. Then he put his cleats into his bag, got up, and left without saying a word to anybody. I shoved my feet into my shoes, grabbed my clothes, bundled them up into a ball, and ran out after him.

"Steve!" I yelled down the hall.

He stopped and turned around. He nodded, but there was no smile.

"Pretty rough morning after last night," I said.

"I don't even want to think about last night," he said. "Not our finest moment."

"I was sort of wanting to talk to you about what happened."

He looked around. There were people all around. "Not here."

He walked down the hall and I trailed after him. We headed out the door and didn't stop until we were standing alone on the track.

"What do you want to talk about?"

"I don't know…it just really bothered me."

He laughed, but it wasn't a happy laugh. "Join the club. It just got out of control."

"The eggs were one thing. But the pots...that smashed window."

"I couldn't get that out of my mind last night," Steve said. "I felt bad. She didn't deserve that and neither did her family."

"She? Whose house was it?"

"That girl...the one Kevin was arguing with."

"What girl?"

"The one from yesterday. The one with the black *burka*."

"Zana," I gasped. "That was Zana's house?"

"Keep your voice down," he snapped.

I couldn't help but picture Zana and Haroon inside the house. Were their parents there? Did they have other brothers and sisters? Was anybody hurt?

"I didn't know," I said.

"Me neither. After he dropped you and Junior off, it was just him and me. He started to go on about her being a stinking sand monkey and teaching her a lesson." Steve shook his head slowly. "Do you realize that fifty years ago there would have been a mob outside my grandfather's house, throwing bricks through *his* window? Actually, my Swedish grandfather would have been tossing bricks at my *father*! Forget tossing rice at the bride and groom—it would have been rocks at the groom." Steve shook his head slowly. "And there I was doing the same thing to somebody else." Steve

249

looked even more miserable than I felt. He looked like he was going to cry.

I put my hand on his shoulder. "You didn't know. *We* didn't know."

"Still doesn't make it right." He looked up at me. "Nothing we can do to make it right."

"I just wish I could forget the whole thing ever happened."

"So do I," Steve said.

"At least it's over."

"Maybe it is, maybe it isn't."

"What do you mean?"

"They would have called the police," Steve said. "Police will investigate. Someone at school will figure it out. Doesn't take many brains to put two and two together."

"I don't understand."

"The attacks were on the football coach of another school, a teacher who gave football players a hard time, a former principal of this school—and I'm sure Zana hasn't forgotten what happened between her and Kevin."

I hadn't thought of any of that. Maybe *I* didn't have enough brains to put it all together.

"If we get questioned we all have to stick to the story. As awful as that is, we have to stick together," Steve said. "Nobody can prove anything if we don't admit to it."

I hadn't thought much about the alibi. I'd just thought that it was Kevin being careful—being a quarterback and looking for a secondary receiver. I never dreamed that we might actually have to lie to somebody. But to whom? Our parents, the principal...the police?

"I don't feel any better about it than you do," Steve said. "But what good would telling do? It wouldn't change the trouble we've caused. It would only mean more trouble for all of us, right?"

Reluctantly I nodded.

"We're a team. We have to stick together," Steve said. "See you at lunch."

He took a few steps, stopped, and turned to face me. "I'm glad it isn't just me feeling this way."

Then he walked away.

CHAPTER TWENTY-FIVE

HAROON

I FEEL LIKE MAKING a grand gesture, something that shows everyone I'm not afraid of being afraid. But early morning wisdom and heroic thoughts stall and stumble against the reality and routine of high school. I'm not a grand gesture sort of person. Zana certainly is. I'm more of a go-along-to-get-along sort. I'm the sort of person who would start something heroic, feel conspicuous halfway through, and then slink away, apologizing.

Still, we won the match last night. Maybe I'm not as much of a slinker as I thought I was.

It's in algebra class that I get an idea. The teacher has moved on to something new that I *could* follow— thanks to Azeem's recent coaching—but only if I were concentrating hard, which I'm not today. I'll do dishes for Zana later in exchange for her explaining it to me. Taking advantage of my new high status as a *Reach for the Top* winner—however fleeting that will be—I go to the board when we're supposed to be working on an exercise. I pick up the chalk, and write six words.

Fear of Terror. Terror of Fear.

I go back to my seat. I can see the class reading the words, thinking about them. My teacher too. Then the thread of the lesson is picked up, and we go back to work.

I do the same in my next class, and the next. It's not exactly a grand gesture, but maybe it will make some people think.

At lunchtime, Julian and I are walking around outside. It's a warm day, for November, and a lot of kids are hanging around.

"Where's Reverend Bob?" I ask.

"*Sister* Bob was a naughty nun last night," Julian says. "She danced so much, her head fell off. She's in the little nun's hospital."

"Good party?"

"The best. Sorry you couldn't make it."

"Next time. I promise." Next Halloween is a whole year away. Hopefully, Julian will forget.

"Next time? You heard that, everybody! Big Brain Haroon will be the featured attraction at the Snowflake Ball this December. Only six weeks away! Get your tickets now!"

I try to stop him, but there's no stopping Julian. I can see I'm going to have to start thinking of where to borrow a dress. Mom's won't fit me, and she mostly wears trousers, anyway.

I see a stray ball in the weeds against the school

wall and pick it up. Julian and I toss it back and forth as we walk, then I see Zana standing with some of her veiled friends. I can recognize her, now. I'm getting used to her being dressed like that, and I can see beyond the yards of black cloth to posture, movement, and energy.

"Hey! Zana!" I yell. She turns, and I toss her the ball. She catches it without effort, and soon Julian and I are playing catch with four veiled women. As we laugh and jump and run, I can see the reactions of students outside our circle. Can Muslim women really laugh, run, fumble the ball, and toss it in a perfect arc, just like the rest of us?

Some of them join in. Our circle expands. I toss the ball to someone I don't know, just another kid, who tosses it back across the circle to one of Zana's friends.

Fear of terror? Not here, I think. For this great and glorious moment, not here.

CHAPTER TWENTY-SIX

JAY

"COULD THE MEMBERS of the football team please report to the office—*immediately.*"

I felt my whole body stiffen before the announcement had even ended. Announcements made by Mrs. Willis were never about good things. And there was something about the tone of her voice that told me it was going to be really, really bad.

Slowly I gathered up all my books and stuffed them in my bag.

"You can leave your things," Mrs. Higgins said. "The class has hardly started. You'll be back before the period is up."

"Better if I just take them. Just in case."

Just in case it took the rest of the period. Just in case it took longer.

As I stood up, every eye in the class was on me. I felt like everybody knew. It seemed like half the kids in the school had already heard about last night. It was the talk in the halls, the buzz around the whole school. I closed the door quietly. The halls were empty. Then another door opened and another member of the team came into the hall. He nodded at me.

"Do you think this is about last night?" he asked as we started down the hall.

"I don't know."

"Me neither. I'm just glad I don't know nothin' about last night," he said.

He hadn't been with us. Lucky guy.

"You know anything?" he asked.

"Me? Nothing except what I heard this morning," I lied. That wasn't so hard.

"People are talking. They think it has to do with the football team," he said. "I hope that's wrong. Anybody involved will be suspended, maybe even expelled. We can't afford to lose any key players. You know…like the quarterback."

"Why would you think Kevin was involved?"

"Like I said, I don't know nothin'. Knowing nothin' don't mean I can't think. Not that I'm going to say anything to anybody."

"Maybe this isn't even about that," I suggested.

"You're right. It could be something else. It really could be."

Turned out he was wrong.

— ✳ —

It was a good thing I'd taken my books. It was beginning to look like I should have taken my lunch as well. After we were all told that this was about the attacks the night before, we sat on chairs in the hall outside the office. We were arranged in alphabetical order, and we were to be questioned separately. At first, I hadn't thought much about it—I just figured that it was a way to sort us. Then I started to think that it had more to do with separating us, making sure that people wouldn't have any more time to plan or talk things over.

We sat there through class change as students funneled through the halls. Some of the kids joked with us; others tried to pretend they didn't see us. Some of them seemed to be getting some pleasure from our pain. They enjoyed seeing the football team called out.

Having the last name *Watson* meant that I was the third last person in line for an interview. Being a *W* sometimes sucked. This time I was happy. Not necessarily happy to have to sit in the hall and wait on display, but I just figured it was better to be here than in the principal's office.

Besides, this gave everybody else a chance to break down first. If they didn't break, I couldn't. I also thought that maybe this whole process might wear the principal and vice-principal down. By the time they got to me, they'd be tired. Either that or be desperate to find the truth and really give me the third degree.

Now I wasn't so good about waiting.

Finally, it was down to me. The door to the principal's office opened and James stepped out. He looked unruffled. As he walked by, he held his hand in front of him—thumb up—so that I could see it but the principal and vice-principal could not.

"Jay, please come in," the principal said. He sounded tired.

I got up and my left leg gave in slightly. I'd been sitting so long that my foot had gone to sleep. I stumbled a little and then recovered my balance. The tingling drained out as I walked. He ushered me into his office and I sat down in the seat beside the vice-principal.

Mr. Atkins took a seat behind his desk. "Let's not waste any time," he began. "You have obviously heard about last night's events."

"Yes, sir. I think everybody in the school has."

"Probably. Some of your teammates think that we are being unfair in focusing on the football team."

"I guess you have your reasons," I said.

"Yes, we do. So where were you last night?"

I didn't hesitate. "I was out with friends, at James's house, watching—"

"A horror movie called *Friday the Thirteenth*," he said interrupting me.

I almost said yes and then realized it wasn't the right one.

"No," I said, trying to stay calm. "It was *Nightmare on Elm Street*."

"I'm not much up on horror movies. They all sound the same to me."

"I don't like them much myself," I said.

Did he get them confused or was he trying to trick me, trap me?

"And who was there beside you and James?" Mrs. Willis asked.

I had to think again. I had no choice but to tell her in order to back up the alibi, but by telling him I was actually naming all of the people involved. Slowly I reeled off the names.

"So there were eleven of you," she said. "There were ten or eleven people believed to be responsible for these attacks. The same number. What a coincidence."

"I guess."

"Jay, do you think that Mrs. Willis and I are idiots?"

I figured that it was another one of those questions I wasn't supposed to answer.

"We know what happened and we know who was involved."

Was this all just a game to them? Had somebody ratted us out?

"All I need is one person to step forward, be a man, and take responsibility for all of this. Are you going to be that person?"

He didn't know. He just *knew*. But without proof, he couldn't do anything.

I shook my head. "I don't know anything."

He took a deep breath. "Jay, you're new to this school," he said. "You get good marks. Your teachers have nothing but nice things to say about you. You couldn't have enjoyed what happened last night. I know you weren't the leader. You're not a senior. You probably just got caught up in things, got swept along, thought that you couldn't say no."

It felt like he was right inside my head. He did understand.

"If you were to talk, if *anybody* were to talk, we'd go easier on them. There's a big difference between a suspension and an expulsion. One is for three days and the other is for good. Is there anything you want to say?"

This part was easy. There was nothing I wanted to say. I shook my head.

He let out a big sigh. "Fine. You're dismissed."

I got up and started to leave.

"Jay," he called out, and I stopped. "I'm disappointed in you."

He wasn't the only one. I walked out of his office. Except for the two guys still waiting to be interviewed, the hall was deserted. I walked past without looking at either of them. Neither of them was involved in last night. Neither of them knew anything.

I felt my breathing become labored. It was like there was something tightening around my chest. I turned left at the exit, rather than right, heading for the door instead of my next class. I needed to get away, to get some fresh air in my lungs.

It was overcast and chilly. It was threatening to rain, but so far, it was holding off. I looked over my shoulder at the security camera over the door. If anybody had been looking, they could have seen me. I circled around the side of the school. I was aiming for the place where we'd gathered last night. Returning to the scene of the crime. At least there, I'd be out of sight of everybody—human and electronic.

I turned the corner and stopped. There was a car parked there—an unmarked police car. The unmarked cars were always so obvious they might as well have had lights on the top and a gigantic sign that read POLICE.

I stepped back so I could peek around the corner of the building without being seen. I wanted to leave, but I was curious. And afraid. Why was the car here? Had they somehow found out this is where we started last night and they were looking for clues? Was this like *CSI*? Were they gathering DNA off the garbage, taking tire tracks? That was crazy. If they were gathering evidence, they'd be out of the car, not sitting inside. There were three of them—two in the front and a third person in the back.

Suddenly the passenger seat door opened up and a plainclothes cop jumped out. I recoiled against the wall, thinking that he'd seen me and was coming after me. But instead, he opened the back door. A person stepped out. He wasn't a cop. He was a kid...a brown kid.

Haroon.

They must have been asking him for details, what he'd seen, if he could identify any of the people involved.

They continued to talk and then the officer got back into the car, and it drove off leaving Haroon standing there by himself. He didn't move. He didn't even watch the car leave. He just stood there, staring at the ground.

I wanted to turn and walk away. The last thing in the world I wanted to do was talk to him. Maybe. I *did* have questions. Was anybody hurt last night? How was Zana doing?

And there were questions that were more selfish. Had the police told him anything? Did they have any clues? Did he see anything? I had to know.

CHAPTER TWENTY-SEVEN

HAROON

"WE'D LIKE TO HELP YOU, Haroon, but we can't as long as you refuse to help us."

I'm in the back of the police car again, "invited" there by Detective Moffett and the other officers detailed to our school. My old buddies.

"By 'helping' you mean accusing," I reply. "I don't know who trashed my house. I don't know who called the bomb threat in to the TV station. And I don't know who trashed Brown Town."

"Would you tell us if you knew?" the officer behind the wheel asks me.

I don't say anything. The truth is, I don't know. I don't know if telling would help.

"We're looking hard here for some kind of cooperation from you, and I've got to tell you, Haroon, you're not making it easy for us."

"I am, actually," I say. "By not accusing people on a hunch, I'm saving you from going after people who may have had nothing to do with it."

Detective Moffett doesn't buy that. "Unless you give us *something—someone*, we're going to have to assume that you're part of it."

"Either that, or you're protecting someone," the cop on the other side of me says, "which makes you every bit as guilty as if you were actually doing something yourself."

"Arrest me, then," I say. "Charge me with something, or quit bothering me. I have nothing to tell you, and I'm done with talking to you. Charge me and give me due process or let me out of this car."

There's a long silence. Then, to my surprise, the door is opened, and I'm allowed to leave.

I step out of the car, and I don't look back.

Standing off by himself, watching me walk away from the police car, is Jay, the football player.

"Why are you looking so happy?" he asks me, as I get closer.

It's none of his business, but I tell him anyway. "I finally stood up for myself," I say.

"With the police?"

"Yup." I grin, I feel so good.

"Aren't you afraid of them?" he asks. "I would be."

"Not anymore," I say. I'm not, either. I refuse to be afraid. "Why are you looking so miserable?" I ask him.

"I just came from the principal's office," he says.

"Trouble?" He doesn't answer right away, so I add, "You don't have to tell me if you don't want to."

"No, it's okay. He talked to everybody on the

football team. He wanted to know if any of us was responsible for what happened at your house last night."

"Why would he think that?" I ask, as we start walking across the schoolyard together.

"I don't know," Jay says. "I guess he has his reasons."

"The police think it was a number of people. They left footprints." I look over at Jay. He's looking kind of pale. "Are you all right?"

"Rough night," he says. "Big party. I think I just need to sit down."

"I know a place," I say. We're not far from Brown Town. There's no one else there, and we sit on the bench. The terrible words in orange have been blocked out with gray. "You okay being seen here?" I ask.

"No problem for me," he says. He starts to look around, as if to make sure no one's watching, and then stops himself.

I laugh. "So, what did you tell the principal?"

He looks surprised. "I told him I don't know anything."

I nod, not really caring. Whoever messed up my house will never help us clean it up.

"Can I ask you a question?" he says.

"I'm the Question King." Then I add, *"Reach for the Top.* Remember?"

He looks blank, then asks, "If you did know something—if you did know about people making bombs, would you tell the police?"

I put my hands in my jacket pockets and stretch my long legs out in front of me. "I've thought a lot about that question. If I knew, I'd tell. I'd tell about plots to bomb or hurt somebody. Hurting people isn't just against the law, it's against Islam."

"What if you found out your friends were involved?"

"My friends or my conscience?" I say. "No contest. But that's just theory, of course. I've never been tested."

We sit in silence for a while, watching a grade-nine gym class pour out of the school to run laps around the track. They look small and young.

"Jay," I ask suddenly. "Do you know who did that to my house?"

For a long while, he doesn't say anything. Then he says, in a voice that's hardly more than a whisper, "I know. I was there."

"Why my house?" I ask him.

"I didn't know it was yours and Zana's. If I had known, I wouldn't have…"

"Would you have stopped your friends?"

"It's hard," he says. "We're a team. We have to act like a team."

"I've never played football," I say, and leave it at that.

"So, are you going to tell?" he asks me.

"No." I wasn't, either.

"Do you think I should?" he asks, then answers the question himself. "I should."

"No, you shouldn't," I say. "What would it help? It would just make more people hate each other more. More anger, more hatred, more problems."

"So, what do we do then?"

I actually smile. "Those broken eggs are really hard to scrub off. We didn't get them all cleaned up before we had to come to school."

I can see Jay thinking, and then he smiles too. "Will Zana be there?"

I roll my eyes. We're laughing as we walk together back into the school.

"He couldn't even spell *jockeys*," I say.

CHAPTER TWENTY-EIGHT

JAY

I STOOD AT THE BACK of the cafeteria, surveying the crowd. Everybody and everything was the way it always was. Everything was normal. Everybody was where they were supposed to be.

Cafrica was in place. Trying to act cool and distant, listening to rap and hip-hop. Off at the back was Curry Lane. If I closed my eyes, I could almost imagine that I could smell the spicy foods that filled all of their dollar-store plastic containers. Somehow, the smell of their food almost matched the music coming from Cafrica.

Up at the front, as always, were the preppy girls. Designer clothes, fancy sunglasses on top of their heads, hair teased and dyed and maximized, push-up bras almost pushing their breasts right out of their tight tops. They were confident, knowing those breasts were both weapons and shields to defend them from anybody daring to defy their position atop the social ladder. Then again, if they were *really* confident, would they need to flaunt it?

Off to the side, almost out the door, sat the emo

crowd. Needing to eat but never feeling like they belonged, even here. And maybe they didn't because they didn't think they did.

Closest to me at the back were the Muslim girls. They sat in ranks according to how traditionally they were dressed. I wondered if it had been hard for Zana to change her place on the seating chart.

The Muslim boys didn't need to dress to impress that they were Muslim. A whole bunch of them wore bandanas or backward baseball caps, basketball uniforms, and jeans hanging down like rapper wannabes. Others were more formal in pressed pants and collared shirts.

Then there were *my* people. Proudly occupying the tables closest to the food. Puffed up, talking loud, taking up more seats and tables than their numbers would dictate. Feet up, voices up, attitudes up. Using their muscles and skills at sports to let everybody know how important they were. That was my spot. My table. I knew everybody who sat at those tables. They were my teammates, my friends, my buddies. I couldn't help but remember how lonely it had been when I first got to this school and didn't have a place to sit. Now I did. I had a protected, safe little haven that I could call my own. But was it so safe? Did I need safe?

Scattered around the cafeteria was everybody else. The band geeks, loners trying to find someplace they could sit where it at least looked like they weren't alone, the new additions, the grade nines still trying to find out who they were, the Goths, the skate boarders, the alternate music freaks, the gangsters and the tough guys and their babes, the serious students, the kids who looked like their parents dressed them, and those who looked like nobody cared to dress them, the odd little ducks, the dirt bags, the gear heads, and the heads—the druggies.

It was a little galaxy with all the planets in place.

Even galaxies have eclipses.

I walked along the side aisle. There were greetings as I got close to our tables. Steve was holding court, making jokes, and generally being himself again. James was beside him, Moose a few chairs down. In the center sat Kevin. If the cafeteria was the universe, this was our solar system.

And Kevin was the sun. Everybody else rotated around him.

Kevin gave me a little nod and took his feet off the extra chair. I had his permission to sit close. It was the place of honor.

I nodded to acknowledge him. And then I kept walking.

I didn't look back, but I could imagine the expressions. Suddenly there was a hand on my shoulder. I turned around. It was Kevin.

"Where are you going?" he asked.

"Just going to sit somewhere else today."

"Come on, Jay." He leaned closer. "I know you're upset about everything that happened. But we're a team."

"We *are* a team."

He smiled.

"And this is lunch. I'm going to sit over there," I said, pointing across the cafeteria. "With a friend." Haroon was standing against the far wall. I raised my hand and he nodded.

Kevin's jaw dropped open. "You're sitting with him?" His face was a combination of disbelief and confusion. I'd never seen that look before. He always looked so confident and sure of himself.

Then he smiled and nodded. "I get it...I get it." He leaned in closer again. "Brilliant," he whispered in my ear. "You sit with him and nobody will suspect us of doing anything."

"Haroon doesn't suspect," I said. "He *knows*."

Kevin jerked back. Now his expression was fear. "But...but...how?"

"I told him."

"You did *what*?"

"I told him."

I started to walk away and he grabbed me and spun me so violently that some of my fries flew off the tray and onto the floor.

"Are you crazy?"

"Let go of my arm, or—"

"Or what? You going to do something right here, right now, in front of everybody?"

I suddenly became aware that we were standing in the middle of the cafeteria, and people—everybody in the school—were staring at us. They couldn't hear what we were saying, and they couldn't know what was really going on. But they couldn't help but see us standing there, toe to toe.

"Well?" he asked. He sounded confident, cocky; like he was sure I was going to back down.

"Yeah," I said. "Right here, right now." I said the words calm and low and slow. I stared him right in the eye, and leaned in even closer—so close that my nose almost touched his.

He let go of me. He backed off a step, smiled, and laughed.

"It won't just be me getting in trouble," he said.

"Nobody is going to get in trouble. He's not going to tell."

"What?"

"He's not going to tell the school, or the police, or his family. Nobody."

Kevin looked relieved for a second. "Why not?"

"You wouldn't understand."

"*You* don't understand," he said. "You're through."

"I'm through with *you*. I'm still part of the team."

I turned and walked away. Haroon was still

standing there, waiting. Balancing the tray in my left hand, I reached out and we tapped hands.

"What happened?" Haroon asked.

"Nothing worth wasting time on. Where do you want to sit?"

"Somewhere in the middle."

I followed him as he threaded his way through the tables and chairs. I knew it was just my imagination, but it still felt like everybody was staring at me—at the two of us.

I hoped they were.

About Deborah Ellis

DEBORAH ELLIS is the acclaimed author of more than twenty books for children. Her work, which often focuses on children marginalized by war, poverty, or disease, has earned her national and international awards.

Among them was the Vicky Metcalfe Award for a body of work. Her jury citation read:

Deborah Ellis is that all-too-rare artist whose deeply rooted sense of social justice is manifest in writing that is lively, lucid, and highly entertaining. In settings as diverse as Afghanistan, Malawi, medieval Paris, and Regent Park in Toronto, her novels chronicle the lives of youngsters faced with enormous challenges.

—Deirdre Baker, Sarah Ellis, and Tim Wynne-Jones

Deborah first gained acclaim as an author with *Looking for X,* her first novel for young adult readers. Published in 1999, it won Canada's most prestigious literary award, the Governor General's Award. She went on to write the multi-award-winning *Breadwinner* trilogy: *The Breadwinner, Parvana's Journey,* and *Mud City.*

While researching another project, Deborah came across the phrase "company of fools." The phrase referred to the small group of people who entertained Black Plague victims in 1348 Paris. Deborah wondered what it would have been like to be a child during that time, and the result was *A Company of Fools,* published by Fitzhenry & Whiteside in 2002.

In the summer of 2003, Deborah traveled to Malawi and Tanzania. There, she spent time with children orphaned by AIDS and the people who care for them. Deborah met a young African girl who acted on a radio soap opera that dealt with social issues. That child became the inspiration for *The Heaven Shop*'s Binti Phiri, a fiercely independent girl determined to reunite with her siblings after their parents die of AIDS.

In her first contemporary novel for middle-grade readers, *Jakeman*, Deborah shifted her focus back to North America, to children whose mothers have been imprisoned. The story follows a group of inner-city children bused through New York State to a Mother's Day visit at a women's correctional facility.

Deborah says of the characters she creates, "Courage interests me—when we have it, when we don't, and how we make the decision to be brave or cowardly. We have created a world where most children live in some form of war, and I write about them to try to do honor to their strength and courage. I have learned that there is no such thing as 'other people's children.' The world's children are a blessing to all of us. They are also our responsibility."

About Eric Walters

ERIC WALTERS has published more than forty-five books for teenagers. A hugely popular author, he has won over thirty awards for his work, including the UNESCO Honour Book for Young People's Literature in the Service of Tolerance. He is a champion of reluctant readers, and he has traveled across Canada many times, presenting to over 750,000 students in school visits. His books have traveled overseas as well, and they have been translated into French, Chinese, Japanese, and Dutch.

In 1993, Eric Walters began his writing career when he was a grade-five teacher. Eric wanted to help his students, many of whom were reluctant readers, become more interested in reading and literature. The result was *Stand Your Ground*, which takes place in Vista Heights Public School, where Eric was teaching at the time. The story also uses many of his students' names and aspects of the local community.

Since then, Eric's popularity has skyrocketed. His name is a fixture in contemporary children's and young adult literature. With best-selling and acclaimed titles like *War of the Eagles*, *Camp X*, *Trapped in Ice*, and *Run*, his output shows no sign of slowing down.

Parents, reviewers, children, and young adults agree: Eric's books are among the most popular in children's literature. As the only three-time recipient of the Ontario Library Association Silver Birch Award, he is proudest of this distinction because it represents close to 100,000 votes from the young readers themselves.

In his many roles as parent, teacher, social worker, youth sports coach, and author, Eric is in constant contact with children and young adults. He draws from these experiences to reflect more accurately the complex world of today's teens. Eric's devotion to family is evident in his writing, and his continuing commitment of teenagers' concerns ensures him a place in children's literature for many years to come.